**JOHN KRUGER** ON VICIOUS KI BUT THIS TIME

He didn't have the US government behind him this time. He had it against him.

He didn't have a terrified witness begging for his protection. Instead he had a beautiful woman too brave for her own good – or for his.

He didn't have an enemy whom he knew. Instead he faced a faceless foe with an army of killers, an arsenal of advanced weaponry and an endless supply of inside information.

What were the odds against him as he stood before a tidal wave of terror about to engulf the world? A hundred to one? A thousand to one? A million to one?

The odds didn't matter. He had to do what he did best. Erase them ...

# ERASER

## A Novel by
## Robert Tine

Based on the screenplay by
Tony Puryear and Walon Green
and story by Tony Puryear and
Walon Green & Michael S. Chernuchin

Ⓢ

A SIGNET BOOK

SIGNET

Published by the Penguin Group
Penguin Books Ltd, 27 Wrights Lane, London W8 5TZ, England
Penguin Books USA Inc., 375 Hudson Street, New York, New York 10014, USA
Penguin Books Australia Ltd, Ringwood, Victoria, Australia
Penguin Books Canada Ltd, 10 Alcorn Avenue, Toronto, Ontario, Canada M4V 3B2
Penguin Books (NZ) Ltd, 182–190 Wairau Road, Auckland 10, New Zealand

Penguin Books Ltd, Registered Offices: Harmondsworth, Middlesex, England

First published in the USA in Signet 1996
First published in Great Britain in Signet 1996
1 3 5 7 9 10 8 6 4 2

TM

The moral right of the author has been asserted

Printed in England by Clays Ltd, St Ives plc

# PROLOGUE:
## THE MAN IN BLACK

**R**oyal Oak could be Anywhere U.S.A. It is a typical American suburban community—middle American, middle management, middle-of-the-road. This quiet, modest suburb is just eleven miles from downtown Detroit, but the calm streets and the tidy houses seem to be light years from the crime and despair of the inner city. However, on that summer night, in a little tract ranch house on a cul-de-sac off North Alexander Avenue, two people, a man and a woman, are being tortured to death.

The sound of a fist striking flesh is a distinctive one; the crack of knuckle against skin and bone a sickening sound as muscle and tissue is reduced to pulp. The four Mafiosi, Paulie Cutrone and his three lower-ranking henchmen, young wise guys sent out to do the bidding of more senior men, had invaded the house just after midnight, surprising their prey as they lay sleeping.

Johnny Casteleone—Johnny C, as he had been known around the Baltimore docks—knew what was happening the instant Paulie's hand closed over his mouth. In a way, he had been expecting this moment for months, convinced of the inevitability—but there was a part of him that hoped that he could elude the long arm of Mafia retribution.

Johnny C had broken the most sacred rule of La Cosa Nostra. He had ratted out his boss, testified before a grand jury and sent made-men to jail. In the brotherhood of organized crime there was only one penalty possible for that crime—a long, slow, extremely painful death.

It had taken only moments for Paulie and Bennie to hustle Johnny C and his girlfriend downstairs.

"Tony," Paulie ordered one of his men, "get to the door. Watch the street."

"Right," said Tony, disappearing into the gloom.

Paulie stood and watched as the other two thugs got to work on Johnny C and Darlene. The man and woman were bound and gagged, then shoved roughly into the living room of the small house, the girl—Darlene—stumbling and falling. Johnny saw the terror in her eyes and felt a stab of conscience. Just before a thick patch of duct tape was slapped across his mouth, he managed to stammer a few words.

"Let her go, Paulie. . . . She ain't nothing to you. What she do? She don't know nothing."

The answer was a hard smack to the face, the force of the blow mashing Johnny's lips against his teeth. He tasted his own blood in his mouth.

"You're right," said Paulie. "She's nothing to me. But she knows you, Johnny. And that's bad. Real bad."

Paulie looked at Johnny for a moment, like an artist stepping back from his easel. He was trying to make up his mind which part of Johnny C's body to attack next. He chose Johnny C's face again, smashing both fists, one-two, cracking bone and tearing skin. Blood poured from Johnny's nose and a white hot pain pulsed behind his eyes. He felt as if his brain had somehow come loose from its moorings and was smashing against the hard bone of his skull.

"You couldn't hide from us, Johnny," said Paulie. He thrust his face up close to Johnny C's. "You shoulda known. Nobody can hide from us."

The young hood stepped back and cracked Johnny C again, a real haymaker of a punch that seemed to start by the floor and ended abruptly on the point of Johnny's chin. He groaned and tumbled to the floor, drifting in and out of consciousness. Johnny C was unaware that Paulie was jumping around the room, waving his punching hand in the air frantically.

"Shit," he hissed. "Bennie! Get me some ice. I think I just broke my fucking hand."

His punching hand out of commission, Paulie slammed the toe of a perfectly polished loafer into Johnny C's breastbone, driving the wind out of his lungs. Johnny's face went very red, then very pale.

"Charlie," Paulie ordered his other goon, "get started with the gas, would ya? We don't have all fuckin' night."

Darlene let out a muffled scream as the thug upended a plastic container of gasoline, dousing her and sprinkling it around the room. As the fumes rose, Paulie leaned down and ripped the duct tape from Johnny C's mouth.

"Just do me quick, you fuck." Johnny C had to force the words out, mumbling through his torn and bloodied lips.

Paulie used his good hand to whip a vicious-looking hunting knife out of his belt. The blade was long and serrated and had been polished to a high sheen.

Paulie leered as he waved the blade under Johnny C's nose. "Do you quick? Sure Johnny, anything you want. . . ." Paulie took a pair of pliers out of his pocket. "But first Mr. Canelli wants a little souvenir. Do me a favor, Johnny. Open your mouth and stick out your tongue. . . ."

Tony, the wise guy guarding the front door, heard the sounds of Johnny C being beaten, Paulie's biting, angry words, Darlene's terrified screams —he cursed at being left out of the fun. His head cocked like a voyeur's, Tony listened avidly. He knew he should be watching the door—but they were in Royal Oak, Michigan, for God's sake. What could go wrong with this operation? What were the chances?

Tony did not have long to enjoy his vicarious kicks. Behind him, the front door drifted open a few inches as if blown by a breeze and he felt the cool of the evening air. Tony unholstered his nine millimeter and peered around the door, looking out into the darkness. Nothing.

But as the hood turned back to the torture going on in the other room, he encountered Something.

Tony never saw the face of the man who wielded the garrote. It all happened so fast he was only barely aware of the flash of a coil of wire slicing through the gloom and whipping tight around his throat. A pair of very strong, very powerful hands pulled him up and back. His neck snapped like dry kindling.

\* \* \*

Charlie had Johnny C's tongue gripped firmly between the jaws of a pair of needle-nose pliers, while Paulie ran the blade lightly along it, as if sharpening it on a barber shop strop.

"Mr. Canelli was very specific, Johnny," Paulie said with a sneer. "He wanted your tongue. You see, he's going to forward this thing to your buddies in witness protection."

Charlie laughed a little too hard. He popped open a plastic bag, ready to receive the bloody organ.

"That's right," Paulie continued. "Mr. Canelli wants your pals in witness protection to take your tongue to the trial. See if it sings on its own."

Charlie laughed again, but Paulie winced. "My fucking hand is killing me." He half turned toward the kitchen. "Bennie! Where the fuck is that ice!"

"Yeah, yeah," Bennie mumbled. "Don't rush me."

Bennie hadn't gotten any ice yet, but he had found a plateful of chicken wings in the refrigerator. He scooped up a couple of the greasy wings and munched on them as he rifled the freezer compartment, pulling out ice trays. He dumped the ice on the kitchen counter and closed the freezer door. As the heavy door swung shut,

Bennie discovered that he was not alone. Rather, he was staring straight into the cold eyes of a grim-faced man dressed head-to-toe in jet black. He was well over six feet tall and almost as broad, and he looked hard and mean.

Bennie stood flat-footed and dumbfounded for a moment, then went for his gun, whipping it out of his belt in an instant. That was as far as he got. He never got off a shot. The Man in Black was a deadly blur of motion, the rock-hard heel of his callused hand slamming directly into the point of Bennie's prominent nose. There was a seismic shift in the bone structure of Bennie's face as the cartilage in his nose broke free of its moorings and shot deep into his soft brain like a stiletto. The Man in Black snatched the automatic from Bennie's dead hand as he toppled to the linoleum floor.

Paulie and Charlie didn't hear Bennie die, but they heard him fall. They paused in their grisly work and looked toward the kitchen.

"What the fuck was that?" asked Charlie.

"Hey, Bennie!" Paulie yelled. "You there?"

There was, of course, no answer from Bennie.

The Man in Black came out of the darkness like a panther, pouncing on the would-be killers. Paulie and Charlie weren't sure who he was—or even *what* he was—but they wanted him dead.

They fired half a dozen shots, a wild cascade of silenced bullets poking holes in the murk. The Man in Black hit the ground, rolling under the gunfire, and came up with his own weapon at the ready. One silenced shot hit Charlie square in the heart, stopping that organ in the middle of a beat. His eyes flipped up and he died, falling as if his legs had been cut out from under him.

There was no clean, painless bullet for Paulie though. Instead, he felt the full weight of The Man in Black as he drove his shoulder into Paulie's stomach, swatting away the hot pistol as the two of them fell. The Man in Black had his forearm across Paulie's throat. It felt as weighty as an iron bar. The delicate tracery of bones in his neck cracked and splintered, his windpipe closing.

Paulie's eyes bulged from their sockets. "Who . . . ?" he managed to gasp. "Who the hell are you?"

The Man in Black looked at Paulie with contempt, then leaned in on his windpipe, putting his full weight on it. There was a sharp crack as the bones in Paulie's entire neck collapsed in like an old building. He struggled for breath for a moment or two, then died silently.

Without a second glance at the corpse, the Man in Black got to his feet. Now his interest was focused on Johnny C and Darlene. The man and the woman exchanged a look of terror—each of them thinking the same thing: Was it possible that a bad situation—a *very* bad situation—could get *worse*? The Man in Black looked a lot more lethal, more dangerous, even more unforgiving than Paulie and all his goons.

Johnny tried to say something, but his tongue was swollen, lolling out of his bleeding mouth. He looked like a baby who needed to be burped.

The Man in Black ripped open the black tactical pack he wore on his waist. He pulled out a small Polaroid camera and a squeeze bottle that looked as though it had once held shampoo.

"Close your eyes," said the Man in Black. His voice was deep and clipped, and he spoke with the suggestion that he was used to issuing orders and having them obeyed without question.

Johnny C and Darlene, however, were too terrified to do anything but gape at him, their eyes wide.

"I said, *close your eyes*!"

Johnny C and Darlene closed their eyes.

The Man in Black aimed his shampoo bottle at Johnny C's face and squirted something on his chin and cheeks. Johnny C jumped and winced as if he had been hit with acid or scalded with boiling water. Then he realized that it didn't hurt. The Man in Black directed the stream to Johnny's upper body, drenching his shirtfront.

Johnny looked down and saw that the material was sodden with something red, something that looked suspiciously like blood.

Darlene struggled against her bonds as the Man in Black sprayed the blood all over her and on the floor around her head.

"Don't move," the Man in Black ordered. "You're dead." He aimed the Polaroid camera and shot two pictures of Johnny C and Darlene. They were blinded by the flash, but when the spots had cleared from in front of their eyes, Johnny and Darlene saw what the Man in Black was doing. Darlene was afraid she was going to throw up behind her gag. Even Johnny C was shocked.

"Aww, jeez . . ." he managed to say around his dry, swollen tongue.

The Man in Black was kneeling next to Charlie's corpse, and with Paulie's knife in his hand, he was calmly cutting the tongue out of Charlie's mouth. The razor-sharp blade sliced easily through the soft flesh. As he pulled the tongue away, he reached for the baggie—still clutched in Charlie's hand—and popped the bloody piece of meat into it. The plastic bag, now filling with residual blood, went into his waist pack. The Polaroids had developed and he scanned them quickly, satisfied that they depicted two gruesomely murdered corpses.

Darlene was still looking up at him, terror in her eyes. The Man in Black knelt down next to her and he whispered in her ear.

"You have three minutes to get cléaned up." He tapped the watch on his wrist. "Three minutes. That's all."

Darlene shrieked behind her gag as the Man in Black raised Paulie's knife, the blade still bloody with Charlie's gore. But instead of plunging the knife into her, he cut through the ropes that bound her. Then he ripped the tape from her mouth, but replaced it with his hand, stifling any involuntary scream.

"I need the clothes you're wearing," he whispered urgently. "I need your watch, your rings . . . all your I.D." Slowly he withdrew his hand. "Now hurry."

Darlene swallowed hard and managed to nod. She backed away a few steps, then turned and raced up the stairs.

The Man in Black sliced through Johnny C's restraints.

"What's goin' on?" Johnny asked, his voice hoarse and still full of fear. "Who are you?"

"No questions," said the Man in Black. "Come with me."

There was a plain, unremarkable, run-of-the-mill station wagon parked in the short driveway of the tract house—just the kind of vehicle anyone would expect to see in Royal Oak. The contents of the car, however, were far from routine.

The Man in Black popped the rear hatch of the car and flipped back a tarp. Johnny C saw that the back of the Country Squire was, tonight, functioning as a sort of makeshift hearse. There were two body bags there, both marked with the stenciled block lettering of the Wayne County Coroner's office.

"Just what we need around here," Johnny C whispered to the Man in Black, "two more stiffs."

The Man in Black ignored him. He grabbed a handful of the vulcanized rubber bag and slung one of the corpses over his shoulder as if grabbing a sack of flour. He cocked his chin at the other.

"You grab that one," he ordered. "Let's go."

Back inside the house, the Man in Black unzipped the bags and dumped out the two dead bodies—a man and a woman, both naked, both rough matches for Johnny C and Darlene.

"Put your clothes on them," said the Man in Black. "And hurry up about it."

"This is getting too weird," said Johnny C.

"Just do it. Now."

As Johnny started his ghoulish task, the Man in Black dragged two bodies—Paulie and Bennie—out of the house, dumping them on the front lawn. Then he tucked the Polaroids showing the "dead" Darlene and Johnny C, along with the plastic bag containing the tongue, into the side pocket of Paulie's sharp jacket. The scam needed one more piece if it was going to hold up. The Man in Black raised the silenced nine millimeter and pumped two bullets into Paulie's back. If no one looked too closely at Paulie's shattered neck, then cause of death would be attributed to gunshot wounds. The Man in Black slipped the gun into Bennie's cold hand, then flipped open a wafer-thin cellular phone. He punched in 911.

He spoke the instant the police operator answered, without hesitation, his voice clear and unemotional. "Yes. There's been a murder at 2322 Alden Drive, Royal Oak. Send the police. Hurry."

The Man in Black turned back toward the house. Johnny C was standing on the threshold of the front door. He had changed into a fresh set of clothes, but he seemed bewildered and disoriented by the lightning-fast sequence of events. It had only taken minutes to go from being as good as dead meat to . . . to what?

"What are you doing?" he asked.

The Man in Black strode past him. "They killed you," he muttered. "Then they turned on each other."

Johnny C gazed at the bodies sprawled on his suburban lawn. In his befuddled state it made sense—he almost believed it himself. "Yeah, right," he said. "Right. Those sons of bitches. That's just the kind of shit they would pull."

Darlene had finished dressing the anonymous female corpse in her bloody clothing. She stood in the middle of the living room, not sure what to do next, wondering whether or not she should trust the Man in Black further, or if she should just run out the back door and take her chances. Her mind was made up for her—before she could act, the Man in Black returned. First he examined the corpse, then he looked at Darlene. In a flash he snatched a diamond pendant from around her neck.

"Hey!" Darlene yelped. "That's mine."

The Man in Black ignored her. He knelt by the corpse and snapped the pendant around its neck.

"Right," he said, "it's yours . . . And from now on, that's you. Do you understand me?"

"Are you crazy?" Darlene was beginning to get her nerve back, as though the theft of her treasured necklace had shocked her back to reality. "You have any idea how much that necklace is worth?"

The Man in Black looked over the glittering stones like a jeweler. "Yeah. It's worth about thirty bucks."

Johnny C cringed as Darlene shot him a withering glance. "You are a piece of shit," she spat. "You know that." It wasn't clear whom she was talking to—the Man in Black for taking her necklace or Johnny C for not doing the chivalrous thing and retrieving it for her.

"Tie up the bodies," the Man in Black ordered. "Tie them up exactly the way you were."

As Johnny fell to the task, the Man in Black grabbed the halfful can of gasoline and splashed some of the liquid around on the floor, emptying it.

Far off, faint but audible, came the sound of police sirens. Johnny C heard them and tensed, looking to the Man in Black.

"Oh, shit! Cops. One of the neighbors musta seen something. We gotta get outta here."

"No one saw anything. I called them." He scarcely looked up from zipping the bodies of Tony and Charlie into the body bags.

"You did *what*."

"Don't worry," said the Man in Black. "This plan doesn't work without an audience." He shouldered one corpse and pointed to the other. "You carry that one."

Johnny C did as he was told. The Man in Black took a quick look around the room. He hadn't forgotten anything. Time to go . . . He pulled a road flare from his waist pack.

"Outside," he said. "Let's go."

Johnny C and Darlene did not need prompting. They hurried out the back door while the Man in Black cracked the flare. The orange-and-blue flame sparked and shot from the tip like a Roman candle. He tossed it lightly, and in a split second, the room was awash in hot flame, the corpses burning brightly in the middle of the inferno.

The Country Square station wagon blasted out of the driveway and rocketed down the street, passing two police cars going in the opposite direction. The cops paid no attention to the car because the house ahead of them had detonated like a bomb—as heat built up inside it exploding through the glass of the windows and tearing a hole in the roof, filling the night sky with fire.

The cops tumbled out of the car, their guns drawn, as if the fire might try to take them down. It did not take the cops long to find the bodies sprawled on the front lawn, illuminated by the fire raging behind them.

"Two dead out here," said one of the cops. "I wonder how many we got in there?"

"Oh, boy," said his partner, "it's gonna be a long night."

In a matter of minutes the Man in Black put a lot of miles between the station wagon and the fire. His eyes were fixed on the dark road ahead, taking every curve like a professional driver and really opening the car up on any piece of straight, level road.

In the backseat Darlene began to cry. Johnny C put a protective arm around her shoulders. "Easy, baby. It's all over. We're okay. . . ." He looked to the Man in Black. "Thank you. Look, anytime, whatever I can do. . . . You really got us out of a jam back there. I want to make it up to you."

There was nothing Johnny C possessed—or would ever possess—that the Man in Black would want.

"Really, man, anything. You name it."

"You endangered your life and the lives of the United States Marshals assigned to protect you."

"What the hell are you talking about? You think I wanted to meet up with Paulie and his goons. I'm betting it was the U.S. Marshals that screwed up." Johnny C knew exactly what the Man in Black was talking about, but there was something in him, a gambler's streak, that made him want to try and bluff it out.

"You were spotted at a restaurant in your old neighborhood," said the Man in Black evenly. "What does that tell you?"

Johnny C knew when to fold his hand. He hung his head. "Yeah . . . Gennaro's. I thought I got away with it."

"You didn't," said the Man in Black.

Darlene looked at Johnny C, her eyes blazing with anger. "What? Johnny—you went back to Gennaro's? That's like going to a country club for wise guys. Are you out of your mind?"

For a moment, it looked as if Johnny C preferred the contempt of the Man in Black to the wrath of his girlfriend. "I'm sorry. . . . It's the osso bucco they got there. I haven't eaten a decent meal in months, okay? I was fuckin' dying. Minga, honey, I'm only human."

"Don't get used to it," the Man in Black growled. "Next time you screw up, you're dead. This only happens once."

The Man in Black brought the station wagon to a halt on a trestle bridge, wrenching the wheel at the last moment to angle the nose of the big car toward the edge, the grille of the car actually sticking out over the void.

"Out," said the Man in Black.

Johnny C and Darlene had learned not to question his orders, scrambling out of the car the instant the Man in Black spoke. Revving the engine, the Man in Black got out of the car, then slammed it into drive, sending the car rocketing over the side of the bridge. The heavy car looked almost graceful as it somersaulted once, then smashed into the water below. It vanished in a huge splash and a great belch of air from its interior.

Johnny C rolled his eyes. "You nuts? That was our ride!"

"A ride from a chop shop. With two bodies in it," the Man in Black replied. "Are you ever going to learn to use your head?"

Johnny C was about to say something until the sense of the words actually sunk in. He closed his mouth.

From the middle of the bridge a pair of headlights blinked on, then died as fast as they had come on. Johnny C and Darlene gaped. They heard car doors opening. Then three figures came out of the darkness.

"Who are these guys?" Johnny C whispered.

"WITSEC deputies," said the Man in Black. "Don't get these people killed. They don't like it. Witness Protection doesn't like it. Understand?" As he spoke, he pulled two white stickers from his waist pack and scrawled two numbers—526 and 527—on them and stuck them on Johnny C and Darlene as if they were nothing more than pieces of luggage to be marked.

Without a word from anyone, the three WITSEC deputies started hustling the two fugitives toward their van.

"You'll never see me again," said the Man in Black. "But I'll know every move you make."

"Wait—" said Johnny C.

"Shut up," growled one of the deputies.

"Use your heads, lie low," the Man in Black continued. "I promise, no one will hurt you. But—"

Johnny and Darlene got the distinct feeling that there was a very, very big but coming. . . .

"You try and skip out on your testimony, I'll give you up to the Canelli family myself. I promise."

"Yeah, yeah," said Johnny, his voice sullen like a child enduring a reprimand from a stern parent. "I got it."

The Man in Black turned and started to walk away. Johnny C wrenched himself away from the WITSEC deputy. "Hey! Stop!"

The Man in Black continued walking.

"Look man, I owe you! I'm a stand-up guy, understand! You ever need anything, you come and see me!"

The Man in Black never looked back. Indeed, he gave no indication that he had even heard Johnny C.

"Hey! You! What's your name."

"Easy, honey," said Darlene. "I don't think he's interested in being pen pals, okay?"

One of the WITSEC deputies led Johnny C back toward the van. It was too dark for Johnny to see the grin on the man's face. "Smile, Johnny . . . you've just been erased."

# 1

There were so many gray, anonymous government buildings in Washington, D.C., that passersby hardly noticed them. For every striking architectural gem like the Department of State or the Hoover Building, there were a dozen more nondescript office buildings, urban wallpaper on the city streets. The Federal Witness Protection Program offices were located in one of these nameless buildings, the anonymity of address eminently suitable to the secrecy of the program it housed. These were not elaborate offices: a floor of cubicles, a photo lab, a print shop, all furnished in uniform, institutional government-issue equipment.

The only unusual aspect of the place was the heavier-than-normal security. The elevator was key operated, discouraging members of the public from just wandering in. If an interloper did happen by, there were two heavily armed security guards—not rent-a-cops—posted at the reception desk. Entry was by I.D. card only, no matter how well known you happen to be, no matter the length of your service.

In the WITSEC offices, the Man in Black was known as the Eraser—and his reputation was considerable—but even he had to present a photo I.D. which identified him by name: John Krueger.

As the Eraser walked through the offices, the few U.S. Marshals who were working at their desks looked up as he passed. Some smiled, a couple greeted him, but they were respectful, their deference bordering on awe.

Some of the older agents, or other members of the Eraser's elite Shadow Operation, were more familiar. Carl Hannon was one of them. He was a paunchy, grizzled old agent. He had been a U.S. Marshal for so long and had seen so much during his career, he was all but impossible to impress. He was sitting on the edge of a desk, overseeing one of the newer agents in the program when the Eraser walked in. Hannon waved him over.

"Hey, John, come over here a minute."

"What for?"

"We need your expert eye. We want you to take a look at something."

Eraser paused, but it was plain that he was reluctant and didn't want to get involved in office chitchat.

Hannon pointed to the younger man. "This is Ray Crawford, John. My new young protégé. Ray, John Krueger."

"How you doing?" said Crawford, his hand out.

Krueger nodded, but did not shake it. "What do you want, Carl?"

"Take a look at this." Hannon put down half a dozen laminated Virginia driver's licenses, fanning them on the desk like a card dealer. "One of these is a fake. We made it in our shop. The others are the real deal. Can you spot the phony?"

Eraser looked down at the licenses and frowned.

Hannon dug a jeweler's loupe out of his pocket and offered it to Eraser. "Here, use the eyeglass."

"Don't need it. . . ." The Eraser ran his fingers over the laminated cards, then tapped one lightly.

"That's the fake," he announced.

Crawford's face fell. "How can you tell? This thing is perfect."

"Is that the fake?" Eraser asked.

"Yeah," said Crawford.

27

"Then it's not perfect, is it?" Eraser walked away.

Hannon and Crawford watched him go. "Who the hell was that?" Crawford asked the older man.

"I could tell you," said Hannon, only half-kidding, "but then I'd have to kill you." He flipped the offending driver's license at Ray Crawford. "Now shut up and run this thing again."

Eraser tried to steer clear of the WITSEC headquarters as much as possible, but the erasure of Johnny C needed one last piece in place before it could be considered complete. He made his way to the computer room in the center of the WITSEC complex, logged on and got to work. It took awhile for him to find what he was looking for in the database, but he did finally manage to come up with a complete set of dental X rays for Johnny Casteleone. Eraser doubted that the mob would bother to check dental records, but he was sure that the Wayne County Coroner probably would. To make sure that Johnny C disappeared completely, Eraser removed the dental X rays and replaced them with the set from the corpse Eraser had taken from the Wayne County Medical Examiner's Office. Now Johnny C was gone forever.

". . . And so, with a little sleight of hand, one very dead John Doe trades places with one very live scumbag. If God were as forgiving as WITSEC, hell would be an empty place."

Eraser did not even look up from the task at hand. "God doesn't have our court system, Robert," he said.

"Let's hope not." Robert Deguerin, a.k.a. Samaritan, was a powerfully built man with a bluff, affable manner, something of a legend in the U.S. Marshal Service. He had also once been Eraser's teacher and confidante schooling his protégé in various arcane arts, but teaching him too well—Eraser was now more skilled than his mentor had ever been. It was a fact of life that both men recognized.

Eraser typed commands into his computer, queuing up his printer. He turned to face his old friend. "Robert, I heard you were getting married again."

Samaritan smiled ruefully. "Yeah, well," he said with a shrug, "I'll just keep doing it 'til I get it right. Marriage is like a tornado, you know? First it's a lot of sucking and blowing . . . then you lose your house."

Eraser laughed. Samaritan dropped into a chair.

"Heard you had a busy night."

This time, Eraser shrugged. "A couple of singers got careless. I had to step in to defuse the situation."

Samaritan pointed to the computer screen. "And that included breaking into the county morgue."

"Someone once taught me that 'improvisation is the heart of field work.' You know, I think it was *you*."

"That was back in the old days, John," said Samaritan. "Things are different now. The weather's changed."

Eraser was an apolitical man. "The singers had to be erased. You know as well as I do that you do what you have to do." Eraser shrugged again. "It's simple."

"No," said Samaritan, shaking his head, "it's not so simple. Now every asshole in Congress wants to chair his own review board and get himself ten minutes on *Primetime*. We have to walk softly now."

The X rays eased out of the printer. Eraser put them in an envelope and sealed it. "Now I get it," he said. "That's why Beller wants to see me. It's about breaking into the morgue, right?"

"No, the old man doesn't know about that. And as far as I'm concerned, he doesn't need to know. It stays in this room. Shadow Ops still has some privileges, I think."

"Thanks, Robert."

"Don't mention it. . . . It was good work, John. I know that."

"I had a good teacher."

Samaritan laughed and said, "Bull shit! You had the best."

Eraser headed for the door that led to the executive offices of WITSEC. "You know, Robert, modesty was never your strong suit."

Arthur Beller had never been in the field, had never even fired a gun. He had gotten to his high position through careful cultivation of the right contacts and by working the bureaucracy, turning every job to his advantage. Men like Samaritan and Eraser did not begrudge Beller's situation, they did not envy him his wood-paneled office and his wall of pictures showing him palling around with presidents and senators. Someone had to play the politics, answer the questions, and get the appropriation for the department. Beller was good at it.

As Eraser entered, Beller handed him a file folder, a dossier, with the full details of his next assignment.

"Fourteen thousand, six hundred and forty-some-odd people we have under WITSEC protection," said Beller, leaning back in his deep leather chair. "But not one of them has a profile like this."

"That bad, huh?" Eraser lifted the security
page on the folder and looked at the photograph
of the subject. She was a strikingly beautiful
young woman—brown hair, smooth brown skin,
stunning blue eyes. She didn't look like the usual
WITSEC profile—they tended to be weasels and
wise guys, not pretty women. But nothing surprised Eraser anymore.

"That bad?" Beller shook his head. "That
good, you mean. This one is a real, live, bona
fide, honest person."

Even Eraser looked amazed. Maybe he hadn't
seen everything yet. "Honest? Then why does
she need us?"

"Ms. Lee Cullen is a senior executive at the
Cyrex Corporation," said Beller. "Ever heard
of it?"

Eraser nodded. "Major defense contractors."

"Mostly top-secret weapons research," said
Beller. "It looks like someone inside Cyrex is
selling out Uncle Sam. The feds need her to
prove their case. She'll be the key witness in
the hottest scandal since Iran-Contra." Arthur
shifted uneasily in his chair. He was enough of a
political insider to know that this case was going
to be a little different from the usual WITSEC operation.

"And when does this go down?" Eraser asked.

"Right now," Beller replied. "The sting is

complete, in place. The minute it's over, she's all yours. You know the drill. Sealed file on the relocate. Your eyes only. Understand?''

Eraser noted again.

''Some serious inside-the-beltway types could get burned on this one, John. It's not going to be comfortable.''

''If serious heavies are getting burned, then it's possible that she could be burned, too.''

''Right . . .'' said Beller.

Eraser looked down at the picture, memorizing those features; his gaze dropped to the block-letter caption beneath. SUBJECT #415. LEE CULLEN. PREPARE TO ERASE.

# 2

**"S**he's in," said Corman. He made a minute adjustment to the focus ring of his high-power scope and threw the figure of Lee Cullen into sharp clarity. He watched as she moved around her office, hanging up her coat, then sitting at her desk and looking through the morning mail.

Lee Cullen knew she was under surveillance, but she didn't bother to look out the window to see if she could spot her watchers. They were there, somewhere, and that's all she needed to know—besides, Corman and the rest of his team of feds were well hidden, even though they were just across the street from the high-rise which housed the Cyrex Corporation.

Corman looked over his shoulder. "She giving us anything yet?"

At the back of the room was a telecommunications monitor attended by a small, furtive-looking man, a Fed irregular, a techno wiz named Dutton. He adjusted his dials, but the snow on the screen remained.

"No. Nothing yet," Dutton reported.

Another agent, Frediano joined Corman at the window and put a pair of binoculars to his eyes. He honed in on Lee Cullen.

"Right, honey," he said, his voice tense. "Check your mail. . . . Now do your nails." Frediano sighed. "Man, I hate working with amateurs. Give me a nice *goombata* any day of the week."

"Hey," Corman protested, "the lady's got balls."

Frediano did not dispute this. He watched in silence as Lee Cullen got up from behind her desk and walked to the large mirror on the south wall of her office. She ran her fingers through her hair, and then fingered a brooch on her lapel, a silver starburst with a large sapphire in the center. She fiddled with the pin, as if trying to set it straight, but in doing so pressed a button on the reverse. Back in the feds' command post, Dutton's monitor burst into life.

"We're on!" Dutton called out. He grabbed his headset mike and clapped it on his head.

Lee's face appeared on the screen, a picture of Lee Cullen shooting herself with the tiny camera in the brooch as she looked into the mirror. There was a minute speaker bud in her ear.

"I look okay?" she asked quietly.

"Tell her she looks great," said Corman.

"Not bad, Miss Cullen," Dutton reported.

"Not bad for an amateur, right?" She was smirking at herself in the mirror, displaying a confidence she did not feel.

"You're doing fine, Miss Cullen," said Dutton.

"Tell her it's time to move," Corman ordered.

Lee received her instructions calmly. She went to her desk, slipped her Cyrex Corp I.D. card around her neck, grabbed a manila envelope, then walked through the plush halls of the executive floor.

The camera in her brooch was still running so Dutton was able to follow her progress down the corridor. "She's almost at the elevators," Dutton announced.

The elevator was empty and Lee Cullen rode the three floors in silence. When the doors swept open on the secure floor, Dutton flinched involuntarily as the camera picked up the security officer parked at the reception desk.

"Afternoon, Miss Cullen," he said. "You here for Station C today?"

"That's right," Cullen replied.

"How long you need it for, Miss Cullen?"

"Ten minutes max."

"Okay . . ." The guard made a note on a clipboard as Lee ran her security card through a scanner. "Sign here, please."

Lee signed and the guard buzzed her through the security gates. The secure floor was where the most sensitive of Cyrex's research was done. Beyond the gates was a warren of laboratories and computer stations manned by earnest techies engaged in confidential research on a variety of subjects. Down here it was all pure science, but the Cyrex Corporation would find a way to turn the discoveries into high-tech weaponry and support hardware. Not one of the men looked up from their microscopes or their video display terminals as Lee passed by. It was an unusual occurrence in Lee Cullen's everyday life.

At a crossroads of corridors, Lee feinted to the left as if going to the Station C file room, but actually went to her right, approaching a door marked MAXIMUM SECURITY—ACCOMPANIED ENTRY ONLY. The corridor was empty. Lee stepped up to the massive steel door and punched a number code onto the keypad.

Corman, Dutton, and Frediano were as tense as Lee. They watched as the vault doors opened silently.

"So far, so damn good," said Corman quietly.

Suddenly the image of the interior of the vault

blurred, then vanished completely, the monitor screen filling with snow and static.

"Shit!" shouted Corman.

"What happened? Has she been pinched?" Frediano looked as if he was ready to run across the street and rescue her.

Only Dutton was unperturbed. "Relax. It's okay. We lose transmission because she's in the vault. That's all."

The two agents looked relieved. "So now what?" Corman asked.

"Now . . . we wait," said Dutton. He checked the fat digital watch on his wrist. "We're at five minutes and counting."

Lee Cullen knew her way around the high-tech cavern of the Cyrex Corp's computer vault, but her mounting tension slowed her down somewhat and she had to fight to keep herself focused and on track. She sat down at the keyboard console and called up the files locked deep in the inner recesses of the brain. A series of small silver disk files appeared, fanning out silently on the robotic system. The FILES TO BE COPIED prompt appeared on the screen. Lee's fingers flew over the keyboard and one of the disks sunk gracefully into the copy bay.

There were millions of bits of information on the disk and even the super-powerful computer took some time to transfer it all. With lightning speed, a series of images flashed on the screen, high-speed graphics, schematics of a futuristic rifle with an exotic tubular sight, specs flashing as the blueprints rotated in three dimensional imagery.

Although it was cool in the computer vault, Lee felt herself beginning to sweat. This was the hard part—doing absolutely nothing, just waiting for technology to do its work. She glanced at the clock—it felt to her as if she had been in the vault for an hour, but she was surprised to find that only two minutes had passed.

The feds were getting nervous, too. They had their eyes locked on the monitor, the static dancing in front of their eyes.

"What's taking so long?" Frediano asked.

"Come on, sweetheart," Corman said urgently. "The shift is going to change before you get out of there."

Lee Cullen jumped when the computer beeped quietly and a new prompt appeared on the screen: COPY PROCEDURE COMPLETE. Lee felt relief pulsing through her. She snatched the disk out of the caddy and jammed it into the manila envelope. She was about to bolt for the door, but she stopped, hesitating for a moment. There was a full minute and a half remaining before she had to get out of there—should she run, or should she copy another disk?

"Damn!" she said aloud as she sat down again and slapped another disk into the port.

**S**he's out of time," said Corman. "That's it. We have to assume that she's been made—"

"Wait!" Dutton leaned toward the screen as the snow cleared.

The camera picked up Lee's progress down the corridor toward the security checkpoint. The first guard had been joined by another, one Lee didn't know. Both men were wary, no sign of the friendliness that Lee Cullen usually got from the lower-level employees.

"Ms. Cullen, Mr. Donahue's office called," said the new guard. "He'd like to see you in his office."

Lee did her best to keep cool. "Okay," she said smoothly, "tell him I'll be up in a few minutes."

"He said right now, Ms. Cullen." The man spoke in a gruff, rather cold tone of voice—it was not the way a Cyrex guard would have dared to talk to her. Unless, of course, she was in serious trouble. Lee had to struggle to keep the fear from showing on her face.

When the elevator came, the guard held the

door open and motioned her in. "After you," he said.

"I can get to Mr. Donahue's office on my own, thank you," said Lee tartly. "I've been there before."

"Sorry, Miss Cullen," the guard replied. "My orders are to take you there in person."

Lee gave a shrug, a little gesture that meant "suit yourself." As the elevator car ascended, she heard Frediano's voice, soft but clear in the ear bud. "Donahue's office? Where is it?"

"Twenty-fifth floor," said Lee aloud.

"I know where it is, Miss Cullen," said the guard.

Back in the surveillance post, Frediano was frantically flipping through the floor plans of the Cyrex Corporation, a book of diagrams as thick as a phone book. "You figure the boss is going to have a corner office, right?" He found the complicated schematics for the twenty-fifth floor and scanned quickly.

Corman was aiming the scope at the high floor of the office tower. "I hope he's not on the other side of the building."

Frediano shook his head. "Got it. He's in the south corner."

Corman spun the scope on its tripod, the entire twenty-fifth floor rushing by in a blur. "Yes!" he said, focusing on the spacious office of the Cyrex chief. He locked on at the very moment Lee walked through the door.

**W**illiam Donahue was one of the best-known figures in the business world. He had taken over Cyrex when it was a struggling start-up technology company that looked as if it was going to get left in the dust by bigger, stronger, richer companies like Raytheon and Teledyne. In less than fifteen years, it had become a hi-tech power-house, a rich and powerful corporation with hundreds of thousands of employees worldwide. Like the other technology giants, Cyrex made all the right public relations moves. It donated money to public television, the "Cyrex in the Schools" program funded inner-city education programs from Maine to Mexico, and the corporation gave money to virtually every charity that came to it hat in hand. But none of this PR could mask a simple fact. Cyrex was in the business of making weapons.

And Cyrex was William Donahue's baby. In the business press, in the columns of *Forbes*, *Business Week* and *The Wall Street Journal*, Donahue was usually referred to as "brash" and "hard charging." Insiders knew that those were merely convenient code words. William Donahue was a take-no-prisoners businessman, a mean, single-minded son of a bitch who would run over anything or anyone who had the misfortune to get in his "hard-charging" way.

Cyrex had a whole slew of senior executives and a board of directors studded with big names from the financial world—from the realms of manufacturing to a few "trophy" directors: ex-senators, retired generals and admirals, even a couple of movie stars.

In spite of all this management, Cyrex operated on a single rule: What William Donahue says, goes. The board of directors was nothing more than an expensive rubber stamp, the directors happy with their large honoraria and the once-a-year golf vacation in Palm Beach in token exchange for voting whichever way William Donahue wanted. Everyone at Cyrex, from the lowliest maintenance worker to the highest executive was afraid of him—even Lee Cullen.

She could tell, from the moment she entered his vast office, that she was in deep trouble. Donahue had no poker face. When he was happy, his ruddy face beamed; when he was angry, it was as black as thunder. Today he wore thunder.

"What is it, William?" Lee asked, determined to play this out for as long as possible.

Donahue did not reply. Rather, he picked up a television remote control on his desk and aimed it at the large TV set fitted into the wood paneling of the office. The set came on and showed a

black-and-white surveillance tape—Lee Cullen
checking the hallway down on the secure floor,
then punching in her number and entering the
computer vault.

She felt a jolt of fear, stronger than the last.
There must have been cameras hidden in the
corridor. What a fool she was for not having
realized that Cyrex would have gone that last
extra step for increased security. Donahue
clicked the remote again, freezing the image on
the screen.

"That's someone I've trusted for five years,"
he said, his voice full of acid. "Someone I as-
sured others could be trusted."

Lee did her best to look puzzled. "I had a file
requirement—"

"Shut up!" Donahue snapped. "We are way
beyond mere bullshit here, Lee. You know that."

In her ear she heard Dutton's voice. "Stay
calm, Lee. We're right with you. Try to get him
to talk. You know what we need . . ."

Donahue leaned forward and looked at her
hard, as if trying to see into her brain, to read
her thoughts.

"Who are you working for?" he asked.

"I should ask you the same question," she
replied lightly. "I used to think we were working
for the United States government."

Donahue shook his head and stood slowly, as

if he was terribly tired. "Oh, come on, Lee. What do you think we do here? This isn't the Red Cross, you know. We sell weapons. We sell things that kill people."

"I am aware of that, William, but we function as the primary research and development contractor for the Department of Defense."

"Yeah? And what do we do if the government doesn't want the little goodies we've cooked up? We're supposed to kiss a billion bucks in seed money good-bye? No. If the government won't buy our stuff, then it's my job to find someone who does. And if I don't, you're out of a paycheck."

"I didn't know that breaking the law was in my job description," said Lee.

"Well, now you do. That's the business we're in."

Dutton, Frediano, and Corman heard the magic words. Without thinking about it, the three men broke into cheers, high fiving all around.

"That clinches it!" said Corman gleefully.

"We got the bastard cold!" yelled Frediano.

The sounds of the celebration echoing in her ear, Lee involuntarily touched her ear piece, then pulled her hand away quickly as if she had burned herself. Donahue eyed her strangely and came out from behind his desk, walking toward her.

"I asked you who you were working for," said

Donahue softly. "I don't think you answered me."

Lee's mind had gone blank and she couldn't think of a word, nothing to stall him, no lie that would send him off down the wrong road. Donahue was scanning her suspiciously from head to toe. His eyes stopped at her brooch.

Dutton, Frediano, and Corman had long since ceased to celebrate. They watched the monitor closely. Each man was holding his breath. Suddenly, Donahue's hand reached toward the lens.

"Christ . . ." whispered Dutton.

That was the last thing they saw. A moment later, the transmission was cut off and snow invaded the screen. Corman jumped to the scope.

Donahue ripped the brooch from Lee Cullen's lapel, the wire and transmitter tearing through the material of her blazer.

"What is this?" Donahue demanded. He stared at the device in his hand. Panic was beginning to grip him. "What is this thing? A camera."

"I'm working for the FBI, Bill. They saw and heard everything you just said. It's all been recorded."

She could see the fear in his eyes and feel his sense of betrayal. Donahue dropped the brooch and the tangle of wires and walked slowly back to his desk. "Oh, Lee," he said, shaking his head wearily.

"They're watching us right now, Bill."

Donahue looked up, his eyes bright with anger. "And you think that makes you safe?" He threw open a drawer and pulled out a pistol, aiming at her. "Nobody's safe, Lee."

Lee's gaze locked on the gun, unable to shift away. "Bill, don't make things worse. . . ."

But to Donahue nothing could be worse. He saw his future unspool like a movie. The disgrace, the trial, the headlines, ruin, jail. "How could you do this to me, Lee? How could you? My wife, my children . . . do you realize what you've done? Do you realize what's going to happen now?"

His hand trembled as he cocked the gun. He spoke in a hoarse whisper. "I hope you understand, Lee. But you've left me no other choice."

He swung the gun away from Lee and placed the barrel in his own mouth and pulled the trigger. The single shot ripped through Donahue's brain and exited through the back of his skull. The slug continued on and shattered the plate-glass window behind the desk. It was like puncturing the skin of an aircraft. The single shattered window opened up the sealed office tower, a rush of wind blasting through the room. Lee was buffeted by the blast as papers, couch pillows, and curtains were sucked out into the sky above suburban Virginia.

Donahue was sitting upright in his chair, blood pouring from his mouth and nose. His eyes seemed to look straight at Lee. The dead gaze held her rooted to the spot. She couldn't move, not even when the security guard stationed outside Donahue's door came bursting into the room.

He stopped and gaped. "Jesus Christ! Miss Cullen, what happened?"

"He shot himself." Lee said, still stunned, still in shock.

"Oh, my God!" the guard shouted. "Call an ambulance!"

Secretaries, executives, and other security guards were pushing into the room. Somehow, Lee shook herself out of her sluggishness. As the room became more and more crowded, she managed to squeeze through the door, using the screams and the confusion to escape.

The usually hushed executive floor was full of people now, all of them in some sort of state of panic, like ants on an anthill. Lee walked straight through them as though she were invisible. No one spoke to her. No one noticed her tattered clothing. She pressed the button for the elevator, waited and watched the numbers light above the door, as if it was just another normal humdrum working day.

Lee emerged from the elevator on the ground floor and walked straight for the tall glass-front doors. The guard at the gate had already received orders from the executive floor—no one was to leave the building.

"Hey, wait!" he shouted at Lee. "Miss Cullen! No one is allowed to leave, ma'am."

Lee ignored him and quickened her pace. The guard came out from behind the imposing security console, running after her.

"Miss Cullen?"

She broke into a run—but so did the guard. He ran after her, his hands out to grab her, and just catching a piece of her torn blazer. Lee whipped around and straight armed him hard, throwing him off balance long enough for her to dart through the door.

The guard wasn't put off for long. He scrambled to his feet and raced after her, chasing her down the steps and across the sidewalk. Lee didn't hesitate. She ran straight into traffic, seemingly oblivious to the dark blue van that was roaring down the street. At the last possible moment, the van swerved and fishtailed, stopping right in front of her.

The guard had her trapped—until the door of the van slid open and Federal Agent Corman grabbed her and hauled her inside. The door slammed and the van took off, running a red light at an intersection, leaving the guard just staring after them.

# 3

**S**ecurity was so tight on the Cyrex investigation that Lee was taken not to the FBI Headquarters in downtown Washington, D.C., but to a rundown Bureau safe house on a ratty side street on the edge of Anacostia. It was an old warehouse, drafty and gloomy, the dirty windows admitting no light at all, and naked light bulbs burned night and day. In the middle of the dismal space was a trestle table and a few straight-back chairs. Lee sat in one, facing Sol Leiman across the table. Corman and a couple of other agents, men unknown to her, hung back in the shadows.

Lee was still shaken by the events of the day, her uneasiness compounded by the disturbing feeling that these men appeared to think that she had done something wrong. They didn't come right out and say it, but Lee sensed a silent accusation hanging in the air.

"Now," said Leiman, "let's go over it one more time." Leiman was the federal prosecutor who would take the Cyrex case to court. He was a dour, rather severe man, known for his insistence on dotting every *i* and crossing every *t*.

"Wait," Lee protested, "you haven't answered my question yet. Do you have any idea how close I came to getting killed back there in Bill Donahue's office?"

"We told you there would be certain risks," said one of the agents.

Lee turned her eyes on him. "*You* did not tell me anything. I've never seen you before in my life."

The man smiled slightly. "I'm Special Agent Knoland, Miss Cullen." He jerked his thumb at his colleague. "This is Special Agent Tyrel."

"I was told I would be under complete protection the whole time," said Lee. "And I wasn't."

Sol Leiman cleared his throat and shifted uneasily. "The operation did not go as smoothly as anticipated," he said blandly, as though explaining away a minor glitch. "That happens sometimes."

Lee Cullen laughed at this bit of prosaic bureaucratese. "I'd say that's an understatement, Mr. . . ." she looked at him quizzically. "What's your name? What is it, Leiman? I don't even know who you are."

"Remember, Miss Cullen," Special Agent Tyrel interjected, "you came to us with this."

"I came to you with a clerical error. It was the FBI and the Justice Department that asked for my help."

Leiman nodded slowly. "And we got it. If Cyrex is selling weapons technology, then it is an act of high treason. The disk, the tape, and your testimony will help put the guilty within the company and their coconspirators elsewhere behind bars. You've done a great service to your country, Miss Cullen. Now we have to think of your safety. . . ."

"That would be a first," Lee said bitterly. As she spoke, Eraser stepped out of the shadows and into the pool of light.

"This is United States Marshal John Krueger, Miss Cullen," said Knoland. "He is with the Witness Security Agency."

Lee raised an eyebrow. "And?"

"He'll be handling your personal protection," said Knoland. "From here on in, you are his responsibility."

"My protection? What on earth are you talking about?" She looked from man to man as if they had gone crazy at exactly the same moment.

"Your new identity," said Eraser. "Your relocation. I'll take you through it step by step."

Lee did a double take. "Relocation? What is

that supposed to mean? I'm not going anywhere." She knew, of course, that the federal
government had a witness protection program,
but, like the rest of the public, she assumed
it was for turncoat gangsters and drug dealers
squealing on their bosses.

"Miss Cullen, you're in an extremely high-risk
situation," said Eraser. He shot a sharp look
at the federal agents. "That should have been
explained to you some time ago."

All of the feds ignored the rebuke. "This thing
didn't end with the death of Bill Donahue, Lee,"
said Corman. "He was just the middleman. We
know there are other people involved. Other,
more dangerous people."

Lee Cullen shook her head and looked indig-
nant. "So you expect me to what? Give up my
whole life over this?"

"Just until the trial," said Knoland, as if that
small detail would placate her.

"Just until the trial, huh?"

"That's right," said Corman.

"Then what? I'm on my own, right?" There
was a moment of uncomfortable silence. Then
Lee nodded slowly. "Right."

Sol Leiman did his best to mend fences. "Miss
Cullen, you understand that we do have an interest in—"

"My testimony," she said quickly, cutting him

off. "Not in my life." Abruptly she stood up. "Don't worry, gentlemen, I'll keep my end of the bargain. I'll testify, but that's all I'll do. You can keep your protection. I'm going home."

No one attempted to stop her as she walked away, vanishing into the shadows. They were silent as they listened to her heels clicking on the old concrete floor, followed by the dull boom of the door closing behind her.

"Corman," said Sol Leiman, "put people on her right away or we'll need a seance to get her testimony."

Corman nodded. "Right."

Eraser felt a cold fury rising inside of him. "Who brought her into this?"

"She volunteered," said Tyrel. "She already had a high civilian security clearance—she was a natural. So—"

"So you told her that this operation would be a walk in the park," Eraser finished for him. "You told her you'd be there every step of the way. And now, when she finds out her life doesn't belong to her anymore, it's too late. You guys didn't play straight with her. And now you want her to stand up for you."

It was Sol Leiman who, with lawyerly analysis, cut to the heart of the argument. "Without her, we had no case." He looked up and met Eraser's angry glare head-on. "We had to do it."

"Right," said Eraser, tight lipped. "It's a lot easier to put her ass on the line than yours, isn't it?"

"That has nothing to do with it," Corman snapped, stung at Eraser's subtle suggestion of cowardice. "No one else could get access the way she could. If we could have put one of our agents inside we would have, but you know as well as any of us that would have been just about impossible."

"You have your disk," said Eraser. "You have the tape. Christ, Donahue buttressed your case by killing himself. Why not let her back out now? Before she gets famous."

"How long have you been in law enforcement, Krueger?" asked Corman. "You haven't figured out yet that a real live, living, breathing witness is better than any piece of physical evidence."

Eraser was about to answer when Sol Leiman held up his hand like a cop stopping traffic. "Okay, that's enough. The whys and wherefores don't matter now," he said. "Do everyone a favor, Krueger. Just keep her alive."

**4**

Corman had given Frediano and Dutton the duty of delivering the disk to the evidence archive at the FBI's Hoover Building. The evidence room was a locked-down, secure chamber and the two agents had to go through elaborate security measures to gain entrance. They signed in, had their identification examined at two checkpoints before getting to the evidence clerk himself. He sat inside a locked cage, reading a magazine, classical music playing softly on a small CD player.

"I always think this looks like a pretty cushy job," Frediano said to the evidence clerk.

The clerk laughed. "Yeah, but no action."

"I'll trade you," said Frediano.

"I'm happy where I am, thanks. What you got for me today?"

Dutton handed over the manila envelope containing the precious disk. "Take good care of this."

"Don't I always?" said the clerk. He ripped the evidence receipt off the envelope, signed it and handed it back.

"There you go," he said, tendering the receipt. "Always a pleasure."

The clerk waited until Frediano and Dutton were long gone before he picked up the manila envelope and walked back into the recesses of the evidence vault. On a shelf near the back he kept his small collection of compact disks. He took down a CD case, a recording of Mozart's Psalm "De Profundus Clamavi" and extracted from it a perfect copy of the Cyrex disk, switching this fake for real one. Once the exchange was made, he returned to his post, reflecting—not for the first time—that all this elaborate security was largely useless . . .

Lee Cullen's home in McLean, Virginia, was modest by the standards of that exclusive little town, but it suited her nicely. It was small and set back from the road, the facade of the building obscured by bushes and trees. A calm, private space, a place of refuge after a day dealing with the world of business.

But tonight, after the terrifying events that had unfolded that day, she was particularly glad to be home. She parked her car in the short driveway and almost ran into the house. But she was not in so much of a hurry that she did not notice the nondescript Ford sedan parked across the street, in direct view of the house. The car couldn't be more obvious—a shiny BMW, Mercedes or Lexus would not have drawn a glance, but a beat-up Crown Victoria just wasn't a McLean, Virginia, kind of car.

Once in the house, Lee went to the window and checked to see if the car was still there. It was.

With a frown on her face, she sat down at her computer and turned it on. As the machine warmed up, she dug in her purse and pulled out a powder compact. She took out the pad and pulled out her duplicate disk. She wiped it clean and put it into the D drive of the computer. But when she tried to log on to the data file, she found her access denied. The prompt was emphatic: USE RESTRICTED TO DEDICATED SYSTEMS ONLY.

"Damn," Lee whispered. It was just like the Cyrex mania for security that would require that its most sensitive files be read only on a machine designed specifically for that program. And there was only one of those—back in the Cyrex computer vault. Lee activated the modem and telnetted into the Cyrex computer grid, just to see if she could mirror the functions of the secure computer. It did not come as a surprise that she never got past the threshold firewall.

Her fingers danced over the keys as she logged off quickly. But not fast enough. The Cyrex security grid had detected an intruder and had initiated a trace. . . .

Lee Cullen paced, walking from room to room wondering what to do next. On impulse, she sat down at her computer again and picked up the phone, dialing a number in the District of Columbia.

Claire Isaacs answered on the first ring. Lee could imagine the unkempt woman sitting at the clutter of her desk, a cigarette always at hand and an ashtray overflowing with cigarette butts. Isaacs seemed to be in a constant state of befuddlement, but the disorder masked a razor-sharp mind, an encyclopedic knowledge of the buried bodies of Washington politics, and the courage to publish her scoops without fear. Claire Isaacs was one of the great Washington reporters, with a dozen government-rattling exclusives to her credit.

"It's me," said Lee.

"Jesus!" said Isaacs, exhaling a mighty cloud of cigarette smoke. "Lee? I heard about Donahue. Are you okay?"

Lee nodded. "I'm fine, I guess. But you were right. I shouldn't have trusted them."

Claire laughed her hoarse, smoker's laugh. "Of course not! The feds are idiots. If they weren't, why would they be doing government work? Mark my words, they'll either bury the case or blow it completely." Claire Isaacs took a long drag on her cigarette. "You give me this story and we'll nail Cyrex all over page one. I've had some big stories, honey, but believe me, this is the biggest."

Lee leaned toward the window and glanced into the street. The unmarked car was still there. She jerked her curtains shut.

"Lee? You still there?"

"Yeah, still here . . . Claire, they're watching me. There's a car parked across the street, I don't know what else they may be up to. It may not be safe to talk on this phone."

"I'll be right over," said Claire eagerly.

Lee shook her head and closed her eyes. "No. Don't come. Not tonight. I'm exhausted. . . . Look, I'll call you."

"Wait. Did you do what I told you?"

Lee pressed the button on her CD ROM drive and the tray containing the disk slid out silently. "Yeah. It wasn't easy, but I got it."

Claire laughed. "Smart girl. That's your insurance policy. You go public with this and they won't dare to touch you.''

But Lee was too tired to think about this any more and she did not share Claire Isaacs's glee at the prospect of embarrassing a huge corporation and several federal agencies at the same time.

"Claire, I'll call you tomorrow."

"Stay safe."

She sat at the computer for a moment, looking at the disk, her face illuminated by the glow of the screen. Then she heard something that made her freeze, her eyes glowing wide in fear: There were heavy footsteps coming down the stairs. Her hands trembled as she reached for the phone, her fingers poised above the numbers—who to call?

But before she could dial, a man walked into the room. He was buttoning his shirt, his hair wet from a shower.

"Darryl!" Lee yelped. "What are you doing here! You damn near frightened me to death!"

"Sorry," said Darryl, "I've been waiting for you. I was just getting cleaned up a little."

"What . . . you just let yourself in?"

Darryl walked over to her and laid his hands on her shoulders. "Take it easy, baby. I was worried about you, that's all. I haven't heard from you in days. I wanted to make sure you were okay.''

There was a reason he hadn't heard from her in days. They had been together for two stormy years, an emotional seesaw that swung from passion to loathing, then back again. It had become too much for her, the drawbacks had outweighed the advantages and she had ended it. And an ex-boyfriend was exactly what she did not need tonight of all nights.

''C'mon baby,'' Darryl said softly, ''talk to me.''

Lee brushed his hands from her body. ''There isn't anything else to talk about, Darryl. It's over.''

Darryl smiled that smooth smile of his. ''Now, come on. . . . it doesn't hurt you to say that?''

Lee found herself getting angry. She had ended it and she wanted that to stick. But Darryl was nothing if not persistent. ''It hurt three months ago when I told you I wanted out. But it's been getting easier, believe me.''

''I don't know what you mean, baby.''

Lee jumped to her feet and stormed through the house, Darryl following her. ''You call me six times a day—Darryl, even my secretary hates you. You jam my home answering machine with messages, you leave notes on the windshield of my car. *Now* you break into my house. I'm not kidding, Darryl, it's getting a whole lot easier to stick to my guns on this one.''

"Whoa," said Darryl. "You are cold, girl. You know that? This is Darryl you're talking to."

"Oh, I know that," said Lee sarcastically. "Don't I know that . . .''

Outside one of the feds aimed a sensitive parabolic directional microphone at the picture window of Lee Cullen's house, listening to the angry voices for a moment. He turned to his partner and smiled.

"Lovers' tiff."

"Just not her day, is it?"

"Or yours."

Both feds sat up straight in the seat. On either side of the car was a man with a gun. The long silencers were the last things the two feds ever saw.

# 5

Once the federal agents had been dispatched, the two killers faded back into the night, preparing themselves for the real objective. They put away their 9mm handguns in favor of some real artillery—two of the prototype Cyrex rail guns, weapons of such incredible force they had to be powered by electric packs mounted on each man's belt. These were the guns on the disk. Lee had stolen that morning, not knowing, never even suspecting that these terrible weapons were already in production.

The leader, a burly, ugly man with a livid J-shaped scar carved into the rough skin of his face powered up his weapon and flipped on the X-ray scope. It hummed to life, projecting a basketball-sized disk of phosphorescent green light on Lee Cullen's house. He scanned through the ghost images of the structural beams of the building, bringing the scope to rest on the shadowy skeletons of Lee and Darryl. He locked the crosshairs on Lee.

J-Scar could hear Darryl's voice. He continued to try to talk her round. "Lee, will you just listen to me?" he said. "Just talk to me—that's all I'm asking. That's not too much is it?"

"I'm afraid it is," Lee said curtly. "There is nothing left to say."

J-Scar hit a button on the stock of the gun, switching the magnifying power of his X-ray scope. The green disk homed in on the dark shadow of Lee's heart beating in her chest. His finger curled around the trigger.

But just as he was about to blast away, his companion touched him on the shoulder and gestured silently, pointing to the road. A van had rolled to a halt in front of the house and a delivery man had gotten out. He walked up to the front door with a huge bundle of balloons trailing behind him. J-Scar could read the company name on the back of the man's jacket.

"Let's Party?" he said to his associate. The man responded with an unknowing shrug.

Inside the house, Darryl argued on, unaware of the drama unfolding just outside the front door of his ex-girlfriend's house.

"Things were good with us," said Darryl. "You have to admit that. We had some problems, you know. I admit that . . . but what couple doesn't have problems every so often?''

Lee felt worn down, exhausted beyond words. ''Darryl, please . . . it wasn't working.''

''And who made it stop working?'' demanded Darryl. ''Come on, level with me. You met someone, didn't you? There's somebody else, isn't there? You've traded in Darryl for a better model, right?''

''Darryl, please . . .''

Just then, the doorbell chimed.

''Bet that's him,'' said Darryl, an odd, knowing smile on his face. ''I'll get it. I want to meet this guy. Maybe have a little talk with him.''

Lee knew it was no boyfriend, and she was pretty sure it wasn't Claire Isaacs. Anyone else meant danger. ''Darryl, wait—''

''I can handle him, don't worry, baby.''

He pulled open the door. The delivery man stood on the threshold, his face obscured by the bunch of balloons.

Darryl smiled. ''How lovely, some kind of an infantile gift,'' he said derisively. ''Let's take a look at the card. . . .''

He had barely finished speaking before the delivery man reached and slammed him against the wall. From the middle of the cluster of balloons came a pump-action ''Street Sweeper'' shotgun.

"Hey, what the hell is going on here?" Darryl sounded frightened, the smooth cockiness vanished.

Lee Cullen knew that face. "You!"

In one swift motion, Eraser swept her off her feet and dropped to the floor with her. He pointed at Darryl. "You! Get down!"

"Who the hell *are* you?" Darryl did not move. A split second later, a light like a thousand flash bulbs split the room, blasting through the walls. Something hit Darryl, his chest opening from collar bone to stomach, the force of the impact lifting him off his feet, carrying him along the entire length of the living room, slamming him into the far wall.

Lee was screaming, staring as Darryl's shattered body slumped to the ground. There was a huge, smoking hole in the wall, flecks of flame burning here and there in the room. Keeping low, Eraser darted to the window and looked out. He could see the path the projectile had taken—splintered trees and destroyed shrubs marked the trajectory of the missile across this quiet neighborhood.

Eraser was a realist. He knew he couldn't fight back against whatever it was that they were firing at him. The way to win the battle, Eraser knew, was to get the hell out of that firestorm as fast as possible.

He dragged Lee to her feet, and together they raced through the smoke and plaster dust, making for the kitchen. As they ran, more high-velocity charges blasted through the walls as if they were made of nothing stronger than cheesecloth. The house was rocked to its foundations.

Eraser hit the heavy refrigerator like a linebacker, knocking the big appliance sideways to the floor. Eraser and Lee lay behind it, both breathing heavily. There was a pause in the shelling.

The two killers made their way toward the house, both men scanning the structure through their X-ray scopes. There was no sign of movement in the thicket of shadow images, the kitchen cabinets, the support structure, and plumbing and electrical lines.

"They're in there," said J-Scar. "But there's no shot." The language he spoke was guttural—it was Russian. He took a short-barreled, high-tech grenade launcher from his companion and aimed it at the kitchen window. He pumped the gun once, then fired a silenced projectile through the plate glass. The metal sphere hit the tile, bounced once, and then rolled, stopping as it hit its own weighted disk base. There was a sharp *ping!* as the spring mechanism inside the ball engaged, firing the ball four feet into the air. Then there was a small explosion, like a sharp cough.

Eraser threw open the refrigerator door a split second before the air was filled with thousands of needle shrapnel fragments. The door was riddled with the razor-sharp fragments, one of them long enough to penetrate all the way through the door, the spike driving through Eraser's hand. He winced in pain as his hand was nailed to the plastic interior of the refrigerator door.

They could hear footsteps approaching from outside. Eraser fought the pain in his hand, quelling his instinct to groan or cry out. With his free hand, he grasped his shotgun and pressed down close to Lee.

"Don't move," he whispered. Then he turned his attention to his injured hand. The spike had pegged it tight and he had to work the meat and muscle of his hand around the shaft, loosening and widening the wound enough to slowly slide his hand up the skewer. The pain was intense, beads of sweat starting out on his forehead as he struggled to free himself. He closed his eyes, marshaled his strength and yanked his hand off the spike. Lee felt her stomach lurch and her gorge rise.

There was a crash as the kitchen door was kicked in. J-Scar still carried the rail gun, but his colleague had put away his copy of that awesome weapon, favoring instead the sharp-snouted light assault rifle, a Steyr AUG. The small gun looked flimsy—a lot of its parts were made of press-laminated plastic—but it had an incredibly high rate of fire, high enough to saturate a room in less than thirty seconds.

One of the killers stormed into the living room, looking over the damage and the broken corpse of Darryl. He grunted when he saw him. It had been good shooting, but at the wrong target. Behind him he heard the barely audible creak as a door opened on its hinge. He whipped around and saw, in the shadows, Eraser crouched in the darkened entrance hall.

The rail gun erupted blasting out a missile at half the speed of light. The mirror on the bathroom door shattered to dust. Just as the killer realized that he had shot at a reflection, Eraser stepped out of the doorway and let him have it with both barrels. The street sweeper was low tech compared to the rail gun, but it got the job done. The twin blasts damn near cut the man in half, spraying blood, tissue, and bone chips all through the room.

Eraser vanished, dragging Lee behind him, the two of them racing back to the kitchen. Without heed to the pain in his hand, he grabbed the heavy commercial gas range in a corner of the kitchen and yanked it away from the wall. He reached behind the range and yanked the gas

ROBERT TINE

feed out of the wall. Instantly, the noxious fumes
began to rise in the room with a sharp hiss.

Then he turned and scanned the walls and
found what he was looking for. Using the butt of
the shotgun, breaking the cover off of the central-
heating thermostat, Eraser pushed the heat control up to seventy-five degrees. He jammed his
fingers into the works and pulled out the mercury
switch. Down in the basement, the furnace
kicked in, generating heat in a hurry.

"What are you doing?" Lee whispered.

"Lighting a fuse." He grabbed her with his
good hand; the injured one was throbbing pain-
fully now. "Come on. It's time to get out of
here."

J-Scar and his companion could smell gas and
they had found the shattered body of their other
companion. Things were starting to go wrong.
Both men knew that the men they worked for
didn't like it when things went wrong. Their lives
were on the line as much as Eraser's and Lee's.

J-Scar ducked outside, ready to cut off any
escape while his companion blundered into the
kitchen. There the smell of gas was overwhelm-
ing and he felt that the room was hot. The needle
on the thermostat was almost at seventy-five
degrees, the mercury switch almost level, ready
to tilt. It dawned on the killer that he was going
to die.

The temperature gauge hit seventy-five and the tiniest arc of electric-blue flame spurted from the mechanism.

That was all it took. The house detonated like a bomb, the flames blasting from the ground floor through the second floor and up through the roof. The killer dissolved in a great gout of flame.

J-Scar was lucky enough to have made it outside. He stared in disbelief and he retreated to the street to avoid the falling chunks of burning debris that were pouring out of the sky.

Just then Eraser's van roared into life and blasted down the street. There was no time to fire up the rail gun, so he blasted away with a measly forty-five. He missed. It wasn't his night, either.

**6**

**E**raser was in pain, but it was Lee who was in shock.

As the van raced down the highway, she tried desperately to comprehend what had happened in just the last few minutes. Her mind reeled and she found she had tears in her eyes.

"Are you hit?" Eraser roared.

"What?"

"Are you hit? Are you hurt? Are you bleeding?" He gritted his teeth against the pain of his mangled hand on the steering wheel. "Think!"

"Hit? I don't know. Yes, I'm hit!" she screamed. She was edging close to hysteria, overcome by the terror of explosions and sudden death. "Jesus Christ! I don't know what you're talking about."

Eraser drove with his injured hand and thrust out his good one, leaning over to pat her down,

pawing her breasts and belly like an inept teen-
ager on a first date. Lee pulled away, a horrified
look on her face. She tried to slap away his prying
hands. "Stop it. Stop! What are you doing?"

"Looking for blood."

"Good," she snapped. "Find any?"

Eraser leaned back in the driver's seat, relieved
at being able to put his good hand back on the
steering wheel. "No," he said, "you're fine."

"Fine?" she shouted. "Fine? I am not fine. I
am far from fine. If this is fine, then I'd hate to
hear your definition of trouble!"

"You're not hurt."

"But I'm not fine," she snapped back. "They
tried to kill me. My house has been blown to
pieces. You . . . you're bleeding to death." She
suddenly remembered Darryl's shattered body,
his astonished, sightless eyes. It seemed like
hours since he had been killed, but it had happened only minutes before. She started to cry.
"And they killed, they . . . killed Darryl."

The shock of her ex-boyfriend's death seemed
to overwhelm her. Eraser had to bring her back
to the present. Darryl was dead—there was nothing they could do about that. Surviving—that
was the issue at hand.

"Listen," Eraser said urgently. "You're alive.
That's the important thing. And I'm going to
make sure you stay that way."

"But it was *your* people who got me into this," she said angrily. "If I had never gotten mixed up in this, Darryl would still be alive."

"It's too late to worry about that now," Eraser replied. "You're in it. And you can't get out till it's over. Now, I promise—they won't hurt you. No one is going to hurt you. But I need you to calm down. Understand? If you get hysterical on me, then you're going to make things a lot more difficult. Now, get control of yourself. Understand?"

But Lee did the opposite. Suddenly, she was afraid of him, more afraid of him than she had been of Donahue, even more than she had been scared of the ruthless killers who had invaded her home.

She grabbed the door handle and tried to throw open the door, prepared to jump into the road. Eraser grabbed her and yanked her back into the cab.

"What the hell are you trying to do?" he yelled.

"I'm getting away from you!"

"You can't. I'm all you've got!"

"Why? Why should I believe you?"

"Who else you got?"

Under the circumstances—the highway speeding under her feet, her house in ruins, her job gone, her life in danger . . . she slumped back in her seat and slammed the door. She breathed deep and forced herself to calm down, to focus, to stop her hands from trembling.

"I'm sorry," she said. "I'm not used to this. . . ."

"There's a first aid kit under your seat," Eraser said. "Get it out. My hand is stiffening up. And it hurts like hell."

Lee rummaged under the seat and pulled out a steel box. She searched through it and pulled out disinfectant, some gauze, and a spool of surgical tape. Then she took his large, hard hand in her soft ones, shivering as she looked at the jagged puncture in the palm. It was bleeding and swollen.

"God," she said with a grimace, "that looks bad."

"Just give me the—" He made a lunge for the tape, the gauze, and the bottle of disinfectant.

"No," she said, "I'll do it." She doused the wound with stinging iodine, then pressed the sterile pad into the palm of his hand and wrapped it tight with the surgical tape.

"The thing they used back there, that weapon . . . whatever the hell it was, that was a Cyrex product, wasn't it?"

Lee nodded. "It was an E.M. prototype. It's not even supposed to exist yet. Never mind being up and running."

"E.M.? What does that stand for?"

"Electromagnetic Pulse," Lee explained. "They fire caseless aluminum rounds at almost the speed of light."

Eraser shook his head slowly. He looked disgusted. "Isn't science wonderful? These are rail guns, right?" He had been hearing rumors about these wonder weapons for years—but he had never considered what would happen if they actually went into production.

"Rail gun is another name for them," said Lee.

"I've heard the navy's been working on those things forever. But the smallest one I've heard of is mounted on a battleship."

Lee nodded again. "That's right. The navy came up with the initial concept. Cyrex was contracted to scale them down, to design a compact hypervelocity pulse weapon. The most powerful assault rifle on earth."

"Just what we need."

"Cyrex took millions from the government in research and development; then the company reported that the physics were impossible." Lee was silent for a moment. "That's when I got involved in the investigation. At first I thought it was just simple fraud. You know, someone down the line dipping into the kitty. That kind of attitude exists in the defense industry you know,

'Hey, what the hell, it's the government's money. Who cares . . .?' "

Eraser looked over at her for a moment, then turned his attention back to the highway. "Well, those guns that perforated your house looked real enough to me. Cyrex beat the physics, then decided to sell to the highest bidder. And the U.S. government probably wasn't even invited to the auction."

Lee sighed heavily and rubbed her eyes, as if trying to wipe away the fear and the fatigue. "I didn't think they'd try to kill me," she said quietly. "I just didn't think they would do that. . . ."

"They won't touch you," Eraser said firmly. "I promise you that."

"I'm sure you believe that. But—"

"I believe it," Eraser said. "And you better believe it, too."

"No . . . it's not that. You're just one man. Cyrex is connected everywhere. Department of Defense, the CIA, National Security. Maybe even your people, for all I know."

"Look," he said sharply, "do you still want to put them away?"

"Yes," she said emphatically.

"Okay. I'll hide you until the hearing. No one will know where. Not my boss, not WITSEC. No one."

Lee looked puzzled. "They let you do that?"

"No," Eraser said, smiling slightly. "But I will. The feds knew this was going to be a death sentence for you. They let you walk right into it. They just didn't give a damn."

"I was foolish," Lee said, as if she was partly to blame for the seriousness of her predicament.

"You trusted them, that's all. Now trust me."

The Cyrex computer had detected Lee's attempted access and had automatically started a trace on the line. Once the offender's number had been identified, the machine turned the investigation over to a human. First it notified the security officer on duty that night. Then incident made its way up the chain of command until it was laid on the desk of the Vice President in Charge of Security, Greg Morehart.

It had been a hellish day from a security standpoint—Morehart had been dealing with District cops all day—and this latest wrinkle just compounded the difficulties he had already faced. If Bill Donahue had still been alive, Morehart's next call would have been to him. In the absence of the CEO, the security chief moved up the food chain. He dialed the number quickly, knowing that the private line would be answered not by an aide or a secretary, but by the man himself.

"Yes?"

"This is Morehart. We have a problem."

"Go ahead. This line is secure."

"The Cullen woman has a disk," Morehart whispered. "She tried to access our system with it." Morehart could imagine the man sitting behind his big desk.

"Have you any idea the risk I took to get this back?" The man opened the center drawer of that big desk and pulled out the Mozart CD case. "And now you're saying there's another one out there?"

"We traced the call directly to her phone number," said Morehart, trying to defend himself. "She must have made a duplicate. I don't know how."

"I don't *care* how," the man said angrily. "Just get it. And I don't care what it takes."

Morehart nodded. "Understood. One other thing. We ran her phone records tonight. . . ."

"And?"

Morehart picked up the computer printout. "One call, but it's to a woman named Isaacs. A reporter for the *Washington Herald*."

The man paused for a moment. He looked very grim. "I see. . . . Morehart, I think you know what to do."

Without another word, the man hung up the phone. He sat still for a moment, then popped open the CD case and extracted the disk. He stared at it, then snapped it in half, slipping the broken pieces into his pocket.

There was a soft knock at the door. An army lieutenant leaned into the room. "The Joint Chiefs are ready, Mr. Undersecretary."

The man, Daniel Harper, Undersecretary of Defense for International Affairs stood and smoothed his suit jacket. "Tell them I'll be right with them, Lieutenant."

# 7

High in the mountains of West Virginia, on the slopes of a tall peak called Spruce Knob, Eraser and Lee went to earth. The cabin, buried in the misty fold of a slope, a "holler" in local parlance, could not be seen from rutted dirt road, and the broad branches of tall pines made it invisible from the air. It was Eraser's place, his lair, the most private place in his life, the space he retreated to when he needed to decompress. Few people in the area knew it was there. No one knew the taciturn stranger who appeared a few times a year. The existence of the cabin was unknown to WITSEC.

It was a simple dwelling. A large open room dominated by a tall, rough-stone fireplace, a couple of small, simply furnished bedrooms, and a kitchen. Eraser felt secure and in control when he was there. Lee Cullen could sense his ease and she felt safe.

The cabin had been cold when they arrived. The first thing Eraser did was build a large fire in the grate, the soft, yellow radiance of the flames quickly taking the chill off the big living room. Eraser made a simple meal—soup, some bread— then brewed a pot of strong coffee, fortifying it with a dollop of bourbon. It was time to get down to business.

Eraser got a stainless-steel mixing bowl from the kitchen and held it out to Lee. "Take this."

"What for?"

"I want you to put everything that can identify you in here. Empty your purse. Credit cards, business cards, driver's license, passport, Cyrex I.D. card—anything with your name or your picture on it."

She did not ask why—she knew that she had to disappear for a while. Digging through her wallet, she found a wad of identification, laminated pieces of her present soon to be her past.

"That's it," Lee said, gazing down at the collection in the bowl. "That's everything I am."

Eraser doused the contents with lighter fluid. "This stuff is nothing—just plastic and numbers. What you are is here"—he tapped his chest over his heart—"the real you. No one can take that away."

"Maybe not," Lee said softly, "but they'll try."

"We'll stop them," said Eraser firmly. He pulled a piece of kindling from the fire, a blue flame flickering at its charred tip, holding it out to her. Lee gazed at it for a moment, then took it and touched it to the lighter fluid in the steel container. The fuel caught instantly, the colorless flames burning high and hot. The plastic cards buckled and melted, throwing off a little curl of acrid smoke.

Eraser took the bowl and set it on the edge of the grate. Lee sat on the floor and watched as the pieces of her past shriveled and burned.

"I'll need the rest of it," Eraser said gently.

Lee looked at him, puzzled, mystified. "That's all there is," she said. "I wouldn't keep anything back."

Eraser nodded. "I know you wouldn't, not intentionally anyway." He reached out and took hold of the fine gold chain that encircled her neck. Dangling at the end was a thin gold disk engraved with the figure of a knight in armor mounted on a charger, the lance in his hand piercing the throat of a dragon. Lee grabbed his hand.

"Please," she said, "I've had this since I was a kid." The credit cards, the license, the business cards meant nothing—they were just badges of office adults collected along the way. The medallion was different, a connection to her parents and her past.

He turned the small medal in his hands. Etched on the reverse were some words, worn but still legible. "*To Lee, with love, from Mom and Dad.*"

Eraser nodded. "They would want you to be safe," he said. "That would mean more to them than any gift they've given you."

Tears welled in her eyes as she unclasped the chain and handed it to him. "It's Saint George and the dragon," she said softly. "It's silly but when I was little I used to have these nightmares about dragons. So—" She shrugged and tried to smile through her tears.

"He watched over you?"

Lee nodded.

He glanced down at the medal, then back at her. The gold was still warm from being pressed against her skin.

"Well, that's my job now," he said. Eraser tucked the medal into his pocket. Lee looked away and stirred the fire with a poker.

"Why are you doing this?" she asked.

The response was automatic. "It's my—"

"And don't say it's your job," said Lee. "No one does a job like this for a government salary."

Eraser stopped short, smiling at being caught

out. He was silent for a long moment, and when he continued, his voice was low, confessional. He looked into the distance, speaking as if she was not there.

"There was a woman I knew," Eraser said. "A long time ago, back before I joined WITSEC. She ran a bakery near where I lived. Her hair always smelled sweet, like cinnamon . . ." He paused for a moment, remembering the woman, seeing her clearly in his mind.

"What happened to her?"

Eraser swallowed hard, as if the words caused him pain. "One day some men broke into the bakery. They robbed her . . . and they raped her. In the hospital she told me she knew who they were. She said she could identify them. But she was afraid to testify. She asked me what she should do and I said she had to do the right thing. Testify, I said. The world will never get better if people won't do the right thing. Put them away, I said."

He smiled at Lee. "I was younger. You know how it is when you're young like that. Ideals mean something. And you're so *convinced* you're right, that you know *everything* . . . right?"

Lee nodded. "I know, I know. If you had told me when I was in college that one day I would be working for Cyrex, I would have laughed." She thought about it for a moment. "No, I wouldn't have laughed; I would've been really angry."

There was silence between them. Lee waited to see if he would pick up the story again.

"So . . . she agreed to testify. The men got out on bail. And one week later, she was dead," Eraser said. "And I know . . . I know her last thought was, 'I'm all alone.' There was no one there to protect her."

"It wasn't your fault," Lee said. Her words sounded puny and weak against the strong emotion of his memory.

"If you're going to ask people to be courageous, then you cannot ask them to be courageous alone," he said adamantly. "Someone has to be there, someone has to be there to protect them."

"And that's you," said Lee.

He nodded, then stood. "You should get some sleep. We're leaving at dawn."

While Lee slept, Eraser remained awake, silent in the dark, on guard, vigilant. In the palm of his hand he held the tiny medal, the figure of the knight locked in battle with the serpentine beast glistening in the moonlight and the dying embers of the fire.

# 8

When Lee awoke the next morning, the cabin was still and silent. She rose, took a quick shower, dressing while she was still damp, and then went in search of Eraser. She found him outside. The van was parked in the shed and a Chevy Blazer sat in the driveway. Eraser was bent over the bumper, screwing a set of West Virginia license plates over the original set.

"Ready to go?" he asked.

Lee nodded. "It's not like I have a lot to pack," she said.

"We'll get you some clothes later," he said. "Don't worry. It will be taken care of."

Eraser drove down through the mountains, taking the curves fast, picking up the interstate at White Sulfur Springs and turning north. Traffic was light at that early hour and they made good time, zooming past the small towns of Virginia, clipping a small slice of Maryland, then pushing on into Pennsylvania.

The route took them through the belly of the rust belt, passing the old gray mill towns—Harrisburg, Allentown, Bethlehem. Just before crossing the Delaware River into New Jersey, Eraser pulled the car over and removed the West Virginia tags, revealing New York plates underneath.

Lee had been silent for most of the long drive, deep in thought, her brow furrowed, as if she was working out her future in her mind. Eraser left her to her thoughts, knowing she would speak when she wanted to.

They were deep in suburban New Jersey when she finally roused herself, sitting up straight in her seat. She looked around, looking out the window, as if seeing the scenery for the first time that day.

"Where are we going?" she asked. "I don't even know what state we're in. I lost track after Maryland."

"New Jersey," said Eraser.

"New Jersey?" she said, making the Garden State sound as alien as some exotic Far Eastern realm.

"Why did you change the license plates?" she asked.

"Nothing stands out in New York City like out-of-state license plates," said Eraser. "New Yorkers are always amazed that other places actually exist . . . except for California."

"So that's where we're going?"

Eraser nodded. "There's a place I know there. New York is a good place to disappear."

They took the Holland Tunnel under the Hudson, emerged on Washington Street and turned directly onto Canal. He stashed the Blazer in a parking garage, taking a single suitcase out of the back.

Canal Street led them into Chinatown, the streets crowded with throngs of people. Half of the sidewalks were taken up with vendors hawking a dizzying array of merchandise.

There were enormous displays of mysterious Chinese fruits and vegetables, and live fish thrashing in bubbling tanks. Oil sizzled in woks as food sellers stir-fried lunch for tourists and locals alike. There were mounds of bootleg merchandise—for a few dollars Lee could have bought a "genuine" Rolex watch, a Chanel suit (the label reading MADE IN FRANCE), a Gucci bag. . . .

They left Canal and walked through the warren of side streets. There were shops and restaurants everywhere, few of them displaying signs in English. The air was full of the sounds of people speaking Mandarin, Cantonese, Hakka, Wu, and

Amoy-Satow. Eraser stopped at the door to a tenement building wedged between a Szechwan restaurant and a tiny, one-aisle grocery store.

"Here?" Lee asked.

Eraser nodded. "Here." He opened the door and led her into the dark interior. "There's a woman here I've helped before."

They climbed the stairs to the third floor and stopped before a scarred apartment door. Eraser knocked softly.

The door was opened by an aging Chinese woman, who smiled beatifically when she saw Eraser. She bowed solemnly to Lee.

"This is Mei Ling," said Eraser.

"How do you do?"

Mei Ling bowed again. "My pleasure," she said. "The apartment is ready for you."

"Thank you," said Eraser.

Mei Ling hugged him and then left them alone, closing the apartment door behind her.

The apartment was small, a tiny bedroom and a sparsely furnished living room with a galley kitchen. But it was clean and neat and enough light made it down the airshaft to dispel the usual tenement gloom.

"This is home?"

"For the time being," said Eraser. "Let's hope you don't have to move. If you get compromised, then this place will not be safe."

Lee nodded. "Okay."

Eraser sat at the table and snapped open his suitcase. Inside were blank I.D. cards, fresh credit cards, a hot press, and a magnetic strip maker.

"These are yours," he said. He printed her name on a license and I.D. card and laminated them in the press. "Visa and MasterCards . . . I gave you a triple-A credit rating."

"Thanks," said Lee, smiling. "What's my limit?"

"Enough," said Eraser. "Don't go crazy."

Lee picked up the cards and read her new name. "Lisa Murray? That's me now?"

"That's right," Eraser replied. "You try to match the first name to your real name. Slips are easier to conceal. Last names are always nice and common. Easy for you to remember, easy for strangers to forget."

"You think of everything."

"I try to." He passed her a beeper-pager. "Keep this with you at all times. If the message 911 comes up on the display, you have to assume that your new identity has been compromised. Dump the credit cards, the I.D., everything. Don't try to use them, throw them away. I can always make more."

Lee nodded. "Okay," she said. "Nine-one-

one and I get out of the house. But where do I go?"

Eraser reached into the briefcase, took out a map and unfolded it. "Here. The Central Park Zoo." He circled a point on the paper. "There's a pay phone there. Go directly to it and wait for my call. Anything happens, it's a public place. Six exits, six ways out."

"I understand."

"One more thing." He took a box from the suitcase and handed it to her. The box was small, but very heavy. "Lee, understand that I work alone if anybody comes to you and claims they've been sent by me, works with me— anything like that, use this."

She opened the box. Inside was a gleaming, snub-nose thirty-eight revolver. Her eyes widened when she saw the gun and she looked at him quizzically. "Do I really need to have this?"

"Yes."

"I don't know how to—" Suddenly, the absurdity of the situation struck her. For years she had worked for a major defense contractor, a manufacturer of arms of all kinds and she did not know how to fire a gun.

"It's loaded and the trigger is light, easy to fire," Eraser said. "I know what you're thinking. . . ."

"That I couldn't shoot anyone?"

"Right. Don't think about it. If the time comes, don't think, shoot." Eraser looked very grave. "They will not hesitate to kill you. So you have to beat them to it. Understand?"

Lee nodded and watched as Eraser repacked his bag. "I have to get going," he said.

Suddenly, she felt a stab of fear. In a moment she was going to be alone. "So . . ." she said softly, "I guess I won't see you again."

Eraser nodded. "If everything goes well, no. Believe me, you don't want to see me again."

"At least not until the trial."

"That's right."

Lee searched his face, looking for some trace of emotion. "Thank you," she said quietly.

"Thank me when it's over," Eraser said.

After he had gone, the apartment seemed very empty, the sounds from the street even more alien, more threatening. Lee tried to pump herself up, talking to herself, telling herself that she could not allow herself to slide into despair. She had to stay busy.

Lee went through every item in the apartment, starting with the bedroom. There were several changes of clothing approximately her size in the closet, and a brush, comb, and assorted toiletries neatly laid out in the bathroom.

The kitchen was stocked with plates, cutlery,

and various pots and pans. The refrigerator was well supplied with food and drink. It suddenly dawned on her that she was hungry. She popped a frozen dinner into the microwave, and then turned on the television set, watching the news while her food heated.

The local news—the daily accounting of the havoc and mayhem of daily life in New York City—was just coming to an end. The network news came on and the lead story was Cyrex.

Lee forgot her food, focusing intently on the television screen. A news anchorwoman was speaking directly into the camera. Beside her was a bold graphic: a missile, a tank, and a very large dollar sign.

The anchorwoman spoke in that severe, grave tone that was television shorthand meant to convey that this story was both serious and troubling. "Undersecretary of Defense Daniel Harper spoke today before a Congressional subcommittee regarding the growing scandal surrounding the controversial and secretive Cyrex scandal."

There was a quick cut to Harper facing a phalanx of congressmen. He was flanked by aides and lawyers. Harper spoke forcefully.

"The use of private contractors is totally within the parameters of Department of Defense spending. I, for one, look forward to the Cyrex hearing and I am confident that an inquiry will vindicate my department and prove that there has been no mismanagement of funds—''

Lee snapped off the television set and reached for the phone. She dialed Claire Isaacs's number. The phone rang a dozen times. There was no answer, not even a machine picking up for messages . . .

Eraser took the Delta airlines Washington shuttle from La Guardia Airport and was back in D.C. in time to meet Samaritan at the Orphan's Grill, the WITSEC operatives' favorite watering hole. The place was half empty, the crowd of government workers having returned to their offices, leaving the sparse late-lunch crowd. Eraser spotted the two agents the moment he walked into the restaurant, thin men in dark suits, who sat at a table toward the back of the room, not talking to one another. Eraser knew they weren't local cops and he doubted that they were feds. Samaritan didn't seem to notice them, but if he did, he didn't care about them.

He smiled as Eraser made his way to his usual table. ''Thanks for coming,'' he said.

Eraser was grim faced. ''I don't like to be contacted outside of channels. You know that.''

Samaritan shook his head. ''I don't like them

any more than you do, John. But it wasn't my idea."

Eraser cocked his chin at the two men in the dark suits. "Are those guys with you?"

"Not by choice," Samaritan said with an apologetic shrug.

Eraser had a feeling . . . an uneasy, mistrustful feeling. "Tell me what's going on here."

"Someone has been burning our singers," Samaritan said, his voice low, almost a whisper. "In the last forty-eight hours alone we've had three confirmed kills. Professional, clean . . ."

This got Eraser's undivided attention. "Who?"

"Relax, take it easy, John."

"I asked who."

"Not yours or mine," Samaritan said. "At least, not yet."

"This doesn't make sense," Eraser said. "We haven't lost a witness in years. Did these three break cover?"

Samaritan breathed in deep. "No. That's the problem. . . ."

He didn't have to say any more than that, didn't have to spell it out. Eraser's face darkened. "There's a mole? There's a mole in the WITSEC unit." Quickly a dozen names—fellow agents—shot through his mind. The idea that one of the dedicated men in WITSEC could be turning was almost inconceivable.

"That's right," said Samaritan. "Beller thinks there is. He might be right, too." He nodded toward the two agents. "Our friends over there think so, too."

"Who are they?" Eraser asked. "Federals?"

"CIA," said Samaritan.

This piece of news made Eraser even more uneasy. He had no fondness for spooks, their hot-headed ways and their harebrained schemes. "CIA? What the hell are they in on this for?"

"All three singers were witnesses on high-profile federal cases," Samaritan explained. "Department of Defense. National security. All three cases have international angles. That's the common thread that links the three hits."

"Any other singers in the program that might fit that profile?" Eraser asked. "Anyone we should be watching out for?"

Samaritan nodded. "There are six. One of them is mine and one is yours. We have to live-contact them, uproot, and replant ASAP. There's a jet at National fueling up right now. We have to be on it."

Eraser shook his head. "I work alone. You know that."

"Not today," Samaritan said. "Beller's orders—a buddy system with a CIA escort. Three teams. And we're one of them."

"For Christ's sake! We don't need them."

"I'm not happy about it either, John," Samaritan said apologetically. "But those are the orders of the day."

"Beller isn't trusting anyone, is he?"

"Christ, John, how the hell can he? This is bad. This is the worst it's ever been." He leaned over the table, his voice even lower now. "Look, I don't like working with them, with the spooks. I know them. They like to pretend that they're all buttoned up but they talk more than anybody. . . . For all I know the mole is CIA. Stay on your toes with these guys. We've got to watch each other's back on this one."

Eraser eyed the spooks suspiciously.

"We'll grab my singer first," said Samaritan. "I've got her stashed in a cabin in the Adirondacks."

Both men paused—Samaritan had just broken the golden rule of WITSEC. Never reveal the location of a singer.

Samaritan grinned. "See? I'm trusting you here, pal."

**9**

Two black government cars rolled through a special access gate at National Airport and straight onto the tarmac, making for a corner of the field reserved for private aircraft. Parked beyond the rank of run-of-the-mill Lear jets and Gulfstreams was a Lockheed S-3A Viking, a navy submarine chaser, adapted for civilian use. The two huge engines were already whining, the back draft roiling the air and blowing the carefully combed hair of the WITSEC deputy waiting at the base of the stairs.

Samaritan and Eraser got out of one car, the two guys from the CIA from the other. As the four men walked to the plane, Samaritan did the introductions.

"Gentlemen, this is John Krueger. John these guys are Schiff and Calderon. I forget which is which."

The two men frowned. One said, "I'm Schiff." He handed a color fax photo to Eraser. "You know her?"

Eraser studied the picture. The face rang no bells. "No," he said. "Should I know her?"

"Her name is Claire Isaacs," Schiff said. "She was a reporter doing a piece on Cyrex. We think there might have been a connection between her and that singer of yours."

"Was?" said Eraser. "Someone take her out?"

"She's dead," said Calderon. "But it wasn't clean. Whoever got hold of her went and peeled her like an onion. If she knew anything, they know it now."

"You sure?" Eraser asked.

Schiff nodded vehemently. "I'll spare you the details, Krueger. But it wasn't pretty, trust me?"

The deputy at the stairs rushed forward to meet them. He was new to the service, still a probationer and anxious to look efficient in front of prominent agents like Samaritan and Eraser.

"This is Deputy Monroe," said Samaritan. "He's one of ours. Monroe, you're looking at a legend—John Krueger."

Eraser nodded at Monroe. "Deputy."

Monroe was in awe. "Sir. It's a real honor to meet you."

"Don't believe the stories you hear," Eraser said.

"Yeah, the truth is even more amazing," put in Samaritan. "Tell me what's up, Monroe."

Deputy Monroe consulted his clipboard. "The flight plan is filed for Griffiss Floyd Air Force Base, outside of Rome, New York, sir. And the tower is going to hold outgoing until you're off the ground. You go to the head of the line, first for takeoff."

"That's good, Monroe."

Monroe beamed as the four men clambered up the steel stairs, vanishing into the interior of the jet. He scrambled up the steps after them.

The military guts of the Viking had been pulled out and replaced with a fairly plush passenger compartment. Schiff and Calderon, with the usual CIA contempt for law-enforcement officers, had assumed that they would be flying out on some broken-down prop plane. They were unprepared for the high-tech, luxurious Viking.

"Nice rig," said Calderon sarcastically.

"We've got three of them," said Monroe eagerly. "Very handy for quick relocates. Sometimes they're used to transport violent felons for the feds."

Schiff snorted. "Chauffeurs for degenerates," he said in disgust. "Don't you get tired of baby-sitting scum all the time?"

"Yeah," said Eraser pushing past the two CIA

agents. "But in your case, we'll make an exception."

The top speed of the Viking was five hundred miles an hour, with a cruising speed of four hundred. What with jumping to the head of the takeoff line and a good tail wind, the plane touched down at Griffiss Floyd AFB, thirty-five minutes after leaving Washington, D.C.

A van from the local marshal's office met them, the cargo bay packed with weapons and equipment. Samaritan signed for the rig and the supplies, then took the wheel, driving through Rome and out into the countryside.

"You know," Samaritan said, "this feels strange. Taking three people out to a singer's location. It goes against the training. Monroe, this is probably the only time you'll do this in your entire career."

"Yes, sir," Monroe replied dutifully.

"Don't worry about it," Schiff growled from the backseat. "I'm sure you'll get used to it."

"I'm not worried about it," Samaritan replied. "And I don't want to get used to it." Then, under his breath he added: "Asshole."

They parked on the shoulder about half a mile from the remote cabin and the four men proceeded to get into the SWAT body armor and run their weapons' check. Eraser's preparation was a little unorthodox. He strapped a shoulder holster across his back, checked his huge Colt .45, then slipped it into the leather holster. Then he buckled a combat knife to the inside of his forearm and slid a razor-sharp throwing knife behind the buckle of his belt.

Samaritan unrolled a map of the property on the stubby hood of the van. "Okay, Calderon and Schiff, you go west and take the garage door. Monroe, back door."

"We take the entrance?" Eraser asked.

Samaritan nodded. "That's right. You and me, buddy. Just like old times, right?" He looked at the other three men. "Now we don't need to get shot today, so keep your goddamned safeties on. Okay? Chances are we don't need weapons at all. We'll probably find her inside in her kitchen listening to National Public Radio and baking muffins. Got it?"

"Got it," said Monroe. Schiff and Calderon just grunted. They were used to subverting governments and running spies. Picking up an old lady was nothing more than child's play.

Samaritan pulled a black-and-white photograph from the breast pocket of his flak jacket and showed it around. "Our client's name is Allison," he said. "She's a very nice lady. Let's get her out safely, gentlemen. She gets so much

# ROBERT TINE

as a scratch and you answer to me. Everybody clear?''

The cabin was a typical Adirondack lodge, low roofed and built of pine aged by decades of harsh winters. It was bordered on three sides by stands of tall white pines. The rear of the house looked out over a small lake. Except for the wind blowing through the trees, there was no sound at all.

Eraser and Samaritan made no noise either as they crept up the walk to the front door. The door was open, slightly ajar. The two men exchanged puzzled looks, then quietly slipped inside.

The house was still and silent, so hushed that Samaritan and Eraser knew, through their operative's radar, that something was not on the level. Using hand signals, Samaritan indicated that Eraser was to go left while he himself went right.

Stealthily, Eraser walked down a hallway. He opened the first door he found, encountering nothing more threatening than an empty room, the furniture draped in dust cloths.

But behind him, he heard the faintest creak as a foot fell on an old floorboard. Eraser whipped around. A gunman was slipping into the combat stance, handgun held out in front of him, stiff armed. Before he could pull the trigger, Eraser struck, kicking the weapon from the gunman's hand, then pounding him hard in the face with

110

three bone-crunching jabs. The hard guy went down, his face a bloody stew of bone and ripped flesh.

Eraser sprinted down the corridor to the next door. He stopped there and put his ear against the wood, listening intently. Quick as a flash, the combat knife came out of its sheath and Eraser speared it through the hollow core of the door. The wood split easily, but the razor-sharp point hit something moist and meaty. Slowly, he opened the door and found that he had speared another gunman, the knife blade bisecting the man's face. He groaned in pain.

Eraser put his finger to his lips. "Shhhh," he hissed.

As he shut the door, a third gunman leaped into the hall, his Uzi up and chugging bullets silently. The corridor was raked with slugs, splinters flying like shrapnel. Eraser hit the floor hard, reaching for his Colt. But before he could drag out his artillery, the gunman's head snapped back and an exit wound opened between his eyes. He toppled, his gun clattering off into the shadows.

Eraser looked up to see Samaritan standing at the end of the passage, his gun up the barrel smoking. Eraser nodded his thanks, as if his partner had performed some polite courtesy, like holding a door.

They were standing at the base of the staircase. "I'll go upstairs," Samaritan said. "You check the back of the house."

"Got it," Eraser whispered back.

Samaritan climbed the stairs and ducked into the first bedroom. There was a gunman there, holding a gun to Allison's head, his black-gloved hand clamped firmly on her mouth. Both people seemed relieved to see Samaritan.

"What the fuck you doing?" the gunman whispered. "You aren't supposed to be here until six. You're early."

Samaritan raised his gun. "And you're late." He fired a single shot—*Blam!*—a bullet burrowing deep into the gunman's brain. He fell as if poleaxed, dragging Allison down with him.

"Thank God," she sobbed. "Thank God, you're here."

"Hush now," said Samaritan, his voice gentle and reassuring. "He won't hurt you now."

He crouched down next to her, as if to take her in his arms and hold her close. Instead, he picked up the dead man's right hand, the one still clenched around the gun. Samaritan jammed the barrel into Allison's chest and fired once. The woman's eyes went wide in shock and pain, then glazed over. Her breathing was weak and shallow, blood welling from her mouth with each painful breath. Samaritan pinched her nose and lowered his mouth to hers, feigning CPR.

Monroe burst into the room and stopped dead. "Sir! That's her! That's the singer!"

Samaritan looked up, blood on his lips. "I know that! She's hit! Get an ambulance!"

Monroe rushed for a phone, Samaritan turning back to Allison. "Sorry, honey," he said. There was panic in Allison's glassy eyes and she did her best to speak, to struggle. But she had no strength and it was an easy for Samaritan to put his hand over her mouth and nose, snuffing out her life.

Eraser found Samaritan cradling his dead singer in his arms. "I lost her, John. Lost her . . . Goddamnit."

"It happens," said Eraser. But it didn't happen—at least, it didn't happen to Samaritan. Eraser's mind was working. He looked from Allison and then down to the dead gunman. Calderon had come into the room and was patting down the gunman's corpse, looking for a clue as to identity.

"Nothing," he reported.

"What did you expect?" sneered Samaritan.

Eraser was still thinking. "Why send four men to kill one woman? One could have taken her out easily. Four men someone might notice."

Samaritan carefully laid Allison's body on the

bare floorboards, a tender, sensitive gesture, as if he had really cared about her.

"Someone set us up," Samaritan said, getting to his feet. "Beller is right—someone is talking."

"Hey!" said Calderon. "Got something." He had found a photograph in the dead man's side pocket. Eraser took it. It was a photograph of Lee Cullen, a duplicate of the one on her Cyrex security pass—exactly the same as the one they had burned just the night before.

"Who's that?" Samaritan asked.

"She's mine," Eraser said. "She's my singer."

"John," said Samaritan, his voice earnest and grave, "get on the phone. You have to call her. Now. She's got to run."

Eraser shook his head. "No phones. I have to live-contact her. That's the way it's set up."

"Oh, the hell with protocol, John," said Samaritan angrily. "She could be hit any minute. You've got to get her in motion. Immediately."

"She's too well hidden," Eraser responded. "She's been planted outside the WITSEC loop."

"That's dangerous, John," Samaritan cautioned. "That's really dangerous procedure."

Eraser looked down at Allison and then at Samaritan. "Yeah? Well, my singer isn't dead."

"You don't know that."

"Yes, I do."

"Well, we've got to pick her up and bring her in," said Samaritan. "Where is she planted?"

"Palmer Rapids," he said.

Samaritan looked very puzzled. "Palmer Rapids? Where the hell is Palmer Rapids?"

"Ontario," Eraser said. The lie came so easily to his lips he was unnerved by it. Something, some alarm mechanism deep inside him was kicking in, putting him on his guard.

"Ontario?" said Samaritan. "You mean to tell me you went outside the country with a federal singer?" He shook his head in wonder and disbelief. "You are playing with fire, buddy."

"It's secure," said Eraser. "And the Canadians are friendly people. She fit right in."

"Ontario, huh?" said Samaritan. "Okay. Have it your way. Let's move."

Samaritan led the way out of the room, Calderon right behind him. Eraser hung back, thought a moment, then grabbed the dead gunman's pistol, tucking it into the small of his back. The alarm bell was ringing loud in his head.

While the pilot of the S-3A Viking refiled his flight plan, informing Griffiss Floyd tower that he was outbound over Lake Ontario, Samaritan, Eraser, and the rest of the team loaded the weapons and flak jackets appropriated from the local marshal's office on to the plane. They were airborne a few minutes later.

Eraser said nothing and chose a seat away from the other men. Half an hour into the flight, he got up and made his way to the tiny galley, grabbing a bottle of mineral water from the mini-refrigerator.

"Hey, John," Samaritan called out, "grab a can of Pepsi for me, would you? Thanks."

Eraser dropped into the seat facing Samaritan, handing over the ice-cold can of soda.

"So, Monroe," said Samaritan, "was that your first time under fire? What did you think?"

The young man hesitated a moment before answering—the truth was he didn't know what he thought of his experience. "It—I—" He shrugged. "It's hard to explain I guess. . . ."

Samaritan cackled. "I get it, I get it. I know all about it. Well, it's okay to feel shaky. Tell you the truth, I'm shaky, too."

Eraser took a swig of his mineral water and thought that Samaritan didn't look or act as if he was shaken by the experience. Not only that, he seemed to be taking the death of Allison very well. Had Eraser lost a singer, he would have been crushed with grief and seething with anger, not to mention plotting his swift revenge.

Monroe shook his head. "I don't know . . . I don't know whether to puke or go dancing. It was so terrible, but—"

"Pretty fucking cool at the same time, right?" Samaritan was grinning broadly. "I know what you mean."

"Yeah, I guess," Monroe said sheepishly. He seemed faintly embarrassed at having to admit that he had enjoyed the adrenaline rush of action.

"Come on. It's nothing to be ashamed of. Hell, it's natural. Tell him it's natural, John."

Eraser took another big swig of mineral water and swallowed it down. "It's natural."

"See?" Samaritan said. "The whole game is like that. It's worse than drugs, sex, golf. . . ."

Once you're hooked, there's no turning back. It gets hold of you and won't let go.''

Eraser looked out the window. The clouds were piling up over Lake Ontario and moving inland. He blinked hard and shook his head slightly. His vision was blurring and he felt a strange dizziness stealing over him. He tried to focus his vision, looking down at his bottle of mineral water. Samaritan's voice sounded warped and far away.

"Take me for instance," Samaritan was saying, "my old man was a nobody in D.C., a quiet little guy who drank too much schnapps and who hung out the flag every Memorial Day without fail."

With the exaggerated care of a drunk, Eraser set his bottle of water on the tray table. Fighting the dizziness, he reached behind his back, grasped the handle of the gun he had taken from the murder scene and stashed it down deep between the cushions of his seat and the one next to it.

"Anyway," Samaritan continued, "on his deathbed, my old man pulls me close and confesses that he was one of the men who arranged the poisoning of Franklin Roosevelt."

Monroe looked confused. "Poison?" he said. "I thought F.D.R. died from a stroke."

"You and everybody else," said Samaritan. "But now you know the inside story, Monroe."

"You're kidding, right? Tell me you're kidding." He professed skepticism, but his eyes glittered, excited by the possibility that Samaritan might actually be telling the truth about the demise of Roosevelt.

Samaritan laughed again. "See, there it is. That look. Tell me that doesn't give you a hard-on—knowing the secret world behind the real world. From the day I heard that I was hooked. I ended up in spook school."

Monroe looked surprised. "Spook school?"

"CIA," Samaritan replied. "Yeah, I used to be like these two stiffs here"—he jerked a thumb at Schiff and Calderon.—"and now I'm here. And I'm still a hopeless case."

Eraser was struggling to keep his mind clear. He was more or less sure that he would pass out, but there were things he had to do first. He put his hand in his pocket, his fingers closing around his cell phone. The power came on and he hit the preprogrammed number.

"Of course," Samaritan concluded, "you had to know that my old man was a rheumy, lying son of a bitch."

Monroe laughed and turned to Eraser. "What about you, sir? Why did you join WITSEC?" Monroe peered closely. "Sir? Are you okay? Sir . . . ?"

Eraser stared back, his eyes vacant. Samaritan smiled thinly.

"Speak, O Sphinx," he said. "Tell us the secret thing within thee. . . ."

Eraser raised a finger, his arm felt as heavy as stone. "You . . . you . . ." That was as far as he got. He slumped back in his seat, out cold.

Samaritan was out of his seat in an instant. He jammed his own gun up under Eraser's chin, ready to blow him away if he was faking. Then he thrust his hand into Eraser's pocket, hauling out the cell and checking the display. Samaritan frowned.

"Shit," he growled. "He cleared the number before he passed out. Son of a bitch!"

"Sir?" asked Monroe, completely bewildered. "Could you tell me what's going on?"

"Quiet!" Samaritan whipped around to Schiff who sat at the cabin communication console. "Schiff, did you capture the call he just made?"

Schiff nodded. "Yeah, got it. Two-one-two. New York City."

"Ontario, Palmer Rapids, my ass." Samaritan looked down at Eraser and laughed, amused that he had been taken in by Eraser's ruse. "Calderon, tell the pilot to change course for New York."

As Calderon headed up the aisle to the cockpit, Samaritan pulled the Colt .45 from Eraser's shoulder holster. He had a gun in each hand now. Monroe gaped, still trying to make sense of this scene.

"I'll contact WITSEC," he stammered.

"That won't be necessary," said Samaritan curtly.

"But sir, regulations state that we're supposed to report any change in flight plan," Monroe protested. "This plane is my responsibility and—"

"And a very fine job you're doing too, Deputy Monroe," said Samaritan. "In fact, I haven't given you your official evaluation yet, have I?"

"Sir?"

"Here it is."

Samaritan raised Eraser's Colt to Monroe's chest, the muzzle only an inch from the deputy's white shirt. Then he fired two rounds, point-blank into Monroe's heart. Blood gushed and sprayed. "A-plus, kid. Good job."

Calderon took the Colt and looked at Samaritan's hand—it was spattered with Monroe's blood.

"Yuck," said Calderon.

"Shit," said Samaritan noticing the blood for the first time. "Get me some wet naps or something, would ya? And who do we have in New York? Someone nice and reliable I hope."

"There are four guys from the unit," Calderon

replied. "Reliable. Dependable. And they do what they're told."

"Good," said Samaritan. "Call ahead. Get them ready."

The cabin of the plane tilted slightly as the pilot pushed the Viking into a wide left turn, heading east, making for New York City.

Lee Cullen was sitting in her apartment, dialing Claire Isaacs's number for the fortieth or fiftieth time that day, when her beeper sounded. She felt her stomach lurch when she saw the number slotted on the liquid crystal display. Fighting to stay calm, she grabbed her purse, stuffed in the map of the Central Park Zoo, her beeper, and her gun and ran. She flung her wallet into a Dumpster in an alley off Mott Street. Then, her hand gripping the revolver in her purse, she vanished into the rolling crowd thronging Canal Street.

**11**

**E**raser awoke from his drugged sleep with a start, blinking in the bright, late day. Above the clouds, sunlight came streaming through the aircraft windows. The moment he opened his eyes, the awful realizations came flooding into his brain, hotter and more intense than the light of day. He glanced out the window and saw the jagged New York skyline rising above the low swampland and the high palisades of eastern New Jersey.

The instant he saw the peaks and pinnacles of the Manhattan cityscape, his heart sunk. Now he knew for sure—they knew about Lee, somehow they had intercepted his laconic transmission on his cell phone. He checked the holster under his arm—empty, of course. Still a little bit groggy, he reached between the seats, searching for the gun he had stashed there.

"It's not there." Samaritan was standing behind him. In one hand he held a can of Pepsi, in the other he held the thirty-eight revolver. Eraser grimaced, realizing he was unarmed.

"Oh, come on, John, you can't be surprised that I found this, are you? Did you forget? I taught you everything you know." Samaritan smirked. "The problem is, I didn't teach you everything *I* know." He took a swig of Pepsi, then crushed the can in his hand.

Eraser felt the plane losing altitude. He glanced toward the window. New York City was getting closer with the passage of every second.

Samaritan saw Eraser's look. "That's right, John. We're going to New York. And once we get down on the ground, you're going to lead us directly to your singer. Understand?"

Eraser glanced around the cabin of the aircraft, sizing up his opponents. Schiff and Calderon he knew he could take out if the breaks went his way. Samaritan would be a tough bring down, but Eraser had known that for years. The pilots would have their hands full landing the plane. That left Monroe. . . . Eraser didn't think that Monroe was in on Samaritan's plot, but if he was, he would be easy to deal with. But he was nowhere to be seen.

"Where's the kid?" Eraser asked.

Samaritan shook his head and clicked his

tongue. "Poor Monroe . . . I'm afraid you killed him, John," he said, displaying Eraser's Colt .45, contained in a blood-smeared plastic bag.

"The slugs they dig out of his heart will match your weapon. Your prints are on it. . . . That makes you not only a murderer, but I'm pretty sure Beller and the rest of the world are going to think you're the mole in WITSEC."

Samaritan touched his hand to his cheek and tried to look surprised. "Well, well, well . . . John Krueger, the Eraser, the avenging angel of the Witness Protection Program turns out to be a scumbag. Who would've thought it?"

"No," said Eraser evenly, "it makes you a murderer."

"Ouch," said Samaritan tartly. "On the whole, I think I prefer the term 'businessman.' "

"Businessman?" Eraser said in disgust. "What? Selling weapons with your old CIA pals, right? Or is there more than money involved? Are you and the spooks planning another one of those dirty little wars somewhere?"

Samaritan shook his head. "Naww, John, nothing like that. There's no profit in ideology. We did 'Nam and we lost. We did the Gulf and we won. Win, lose—nothing changes. The only difference is who makes money on the deal. Someone *always* makes money on war, John. . . . And this time it's going to be me."

"You must be pretty rich by now," Eraser said. As he spoke, he eyed the thirty-eight aimed at his skull. "Is it worth it?"

Samaritan dodged the question. "You know," he said, "this doesn't have to end badly."

"No?" This was news to Eraser. People had been murdered in cold blood, federal funds had been misappropriated, arms had been sold—it seemed to Eraser that this could *only* end badly.

"I'd *like* to bring you in, John. All you have to do is give up the woman. What do you say to that?"

Eraser seemed to think this proposition over for a moment. "I say . . . drop your gun."

Samaritan blinked and did a double take. "Excuse me?"

Eraser spoke slowly and deliberately, as if explaining something to someone whose command of the English language was less than perfect. "Drop your gun. Do it now—right now—and I won't kill you."

Samaritan shot a look at Calderon and Schiff. "Can you believe this guy? Excuse me, John, what was that you said?"

"I said I won't kill you if you give up now." Eraser shrugged. "It's really pretty straightforward."

"Wow," said Samaritan. "That's really a hell

of an offer. But I'm afraid I'm going to have pass on that.''

Eraser shrugged again. "Suit yourself.''

Then all hell broke loose.

Eraser reached behind his belt buckle and whipped his throwing knife straight at Samaritan's gun arm. The blade hit its target and penetrated three inches into the meat of his forearm. Samaritan felt a sharp thrust and the searing pain as the knife bit into muscle.

"Shit!'' he said, dropping the gun and grabbing at the blade. Blood streamed down his forearm and through his fingers.

Eraser vaulted over the seats, racing for the rear of the aircraft. Schiff and Calderon had their weapons out and were blasting away, shredding the seats and punching holes in the bulkheads. Eraser hit the rear emergency exit and threw the lever, the heavy door exploding away from the fuselage, blasting away as if the Viking had launched a rocket.

The cabin depressurized instantly, turning into a roaring tunnel of cold, gale-force winds. Eraser was buffeted by the rush of air, driving him half out of the emergency exit, but he held on, snatching at some cargo webbing at the last moment. Calderon and Schiff tumbled to the floor as the plane lurched, Schiff sliding down the companionway toward Eraser. Grabbing a handful of the spook's hair, Eraser slammed his head into the heavy metal frame of the door, knocking him out cold. Then he tore the revolver from his limp hand.

Calderon got to his feet and struggled to stay upright, at the same time firing at Eraser. Bullets perforated the skin of the aircraft as Eraser pulled himself back inside and returned fire. Calderon dove for cover behind a row of seats and tried to reload his weapon as the plane bucked and lurched.

Samaritan was huddled in the galley, wincing as he yanked the throwing knife out of his arm. He looked at the slim blade, considered the damage done—to his arm, to the smooth completion of his operation—and found that he had to laugh.

He peered out from the galley. "John!" he yelled. "I can't believe it. I can't believe you nailed me with this cheap mail-order shit."

Eraser's response was a fusillade of bullets, the hail of hot lead driving Samaritan back into the galley. There was a sudden lull in the shooting and Eraser made the most of it. He leaped up and snatched a parachute rig from the luggage compartment above the seats, then ducked down behind his meager cover.

Slipping the rig over his shoulders and snapping the buckle tight across his chest, Eraser made ready to jump. Samaritan's voice stopped him.

"Hey, John," he shouted, "think about it. . . . Rolls Royce Whisperjet engines with chrome alloy blades. You jump at this speed and you'll go through that starboard engine like shit through a goose."

Eraser paused, his gun still trained on the galley. "You know, you're right." He reached and yanked a jump seat off its moorings in the wall and tossed it out the door. Just as Samaritan predicted, the seat was sucked straight into the massive turbine. There was a bone-jarring shudder followed by the hideous sound of hot metal grinding against hot metal—the engine erupted in flame and smoke, the outer case exploding like a landmine.

The emergency warning alarms could be heard wailing up on the flight deck, as well as the panicked cries of the pilot and copilot as they struggled to control their wounded aircraft.

Eraser slapped the gun back into his shoulder holster, and then swung himself out of the jet, his grip tight on the steel frame of the emergency exit. He could feel the slipstream of the plane tearing at his legs, as if trying to rip him out into the void. He knew he couldn't just let go. He had to make sure that when he launched himself, he fell under the stream of hot metal shards that were pouring as thick as hail off the stricken engine.

Calderon was up and firing again, blasting holes around Eraser's hands clinging to the doorframe. The slugs gouged chunks of metal, coming too close to his fingers. Eraser knew he couldn't wait for his moment. He trusted to fate and let go, streaking through the cloud of oily black smoke and flame. The heat washed over him in a split second; then he found himself in the middle of a quiet blue sky, the ill-starred Viking jet rolling and plunging, the smoke billowing back like a comet's tail. Eraser yanked on the rip cord and the chute deployed, a bright white canopy above him. He found himself enjoying the soft and serene descent—after all, he deserved a little peace and quiet.

It wasn't going to last. . . .

WITSEC hired pilots who knew their stuff, ex-military—Marine Corps for the most part—hotshots who had been in tight spots more than once in long careers of flying. Despite having an engine on fire and the fuselage perforated in a hundred places, the bullets blowing out circuits and relays lining the interior of the thin skin of the plane, the pilot had muscled the aircraft back to level and was engaged in a controlled descent. They weren't out of the woods—not by a long shot—but if their luck held and the plane wasn't subjected to further stresses, they should be able to get to the airport in Teterboro, New Jersey.

The copilot was chattering into his head set, giving the Teterboro tower details of the extent of damage, position, and speed. Samaritan threw open the cockpit door and pulled himself into the cramped space.

"I think we might be okay," the pilot yelled. "If there's no more power loss and the fire is contained, we should be able to make it to—"

Samaritan jammed the warm barrel of his gun up to the pilot's temple. "Turn this thing around!" he yelled.

"Turn around? What? You crazy? We've got a Mayday here! It's a wonder we're still in the air and not spread over half of New Jersey!"

"I said, turn this thing around," Samaritan screamed. "We gotta go back and take that fucker out. Understand?"

"Christ!" the pilot screamed back. "We're lucky to be alive as it is! If I put this thing into a bank, there's a ninety-nine percent chance of us going down. Do *you* understand?"

Samaritan cocked the thirty-eight. "There's a hundred percent chance of your head getting blown off if you don't."

The pilot swallowed hard and gingerly started a wide turn, thick black smoke tracing a dark streak in the sky.

Eraser saw the aircraft bank, then settle, wobbling a little as it leveled off and came roaring back at him. Eraser drifted, helpless, dwarfed by the enormous jet bearing down on him and which seemed to fill the sky to the horizon. The noise of the screaming engines split the air.

When the aircraft was just a hundred yards away from him, Eraser whipped out his Colt, took as careful aim as he could under the circumstances, and opened fire. The first two hits cracked the windscreen of the cockpit, shatterlines spiderwebbing the glass. Eraser's third shot blew the glass in completely. The pilot ducked for cover, dragging the yoke with him as he fell, putting the aircraft into a sharp veer to the left, roaring by Eraser, missing him by only a few feet.

Turbulence hit him like a tidal wave, flipping him over and sucking the air from his parachute. Suddenly, Eraser was plunging toward the ground like a bomb, the chute streaming uselessly above him. He grabbed his shroud lines and yanked out the pins hitching them to his parachute harness. As the silk canopy fluttered away, Eraser looked down and saw that he was plummeting toward a giant auto junkyard, acres of rusting hulks of old automobiles.

Three hundred feet from the ground, Eraser pulled the rip cord on the reserve chute. As he floated earthward, he searched the sky, looking for the ill-fated aircraft, but it was nowhere to be seen.

The small reserve chute did not slow him down all that much, and he hit a stack of junked cars twelve feet high. The sound and force of his impact was like an explosion, old windshields shattering, corroded roofs collapsing. The heap of cars trembled and teetered, threatening to tumble over like a rusty avalanche. Eraser teetered there for a moment until the stack of cars steadied.

On the ground, staring up at him, their mouths agape, were two children, a boy and a girl.

"Hey," Eraser shouted. "Where is this?"

"Earth," said the little girl. "Welcome."

"Those are my dad's cars," the little boy shouted. "You better get off of those cars, man."

Eraser jumped down to the ground and knelt next to the two kids. "Is that your daddy's truck?" He pointed to a beat-up pickup truck parked a few hundred yards away.

"Yeah," said the boy suspiciously.

"You think he'd mind if I borrowed it?" Eraser asked.

The little girl was feeling the silk of the parachute. "Is this yours?"

"You like that? Would you like to make a trade? I'll give you this if you'd let me borrow the truck."

The little boy stepped in and took charge. "No trade. Cash."

"How much?"

"Fifty bucks."

"Deal," Eraser said.

# 12

The WITSEC jet—or what remained of it—sat on the end of the main runway at the Teterboro airport, a smoking wreck, covered in foam and swarmed over by fire fighters and airport personnel. Miraculously, the plane had made it to the ground safely—but it was apparent that it would never take off again.

Samaritan could not care less about the destruction of the plane. He stood with Schiff, the two men poring over a map spread out on the hood of a fire chief's car. Samaritan scanned the map of the five boroughs of New York City, as if Lee Cullen's whereabouts were written somewhere in the forest of streets.

"God help us if she's in Brooklyn or Queens," said Samaritan. "I always get lost out there."

Calderon jogged to them, carrying a clipboard. "Okay," he said reading from his notes, "the call was traced to an apartment in Chinatown, some kind of safe house Krueger set up outside of WITSEC.''

"Yeah? And?" said Schiff.

"By the time the team got there, she was long gone."

"Of course, she was," said Samaritan. "The call was the run signal. That's standard operating procedure. What about the cab companies?"

"Four pickups of solo women in the vicinity in the fifteen minutes following the call."

"What were the drop-off points?"

"Ah . . ." Calderon consulted his clipboard again. "Madison and Fifty-third, Sixth Avenue and Tenth Street, and the New York City Zoo."

Samaritan looked puzzled. "The New York City Zoo? There is no New York City Zoo. There's the Bronx Zoo and The Central Park Zoo. What was the drop-off point?"

"Fifth Avenue and Sixty-first," Calderon replied.

"That's the Central Park Zoo. That's where she is," said Samaritan. He looked down at the map. He shook his head and spoke under his breath. "New York City Zoo . . . what a jerk."

Schiff looked puzzled. "How can you be so sure she's there? At the zoo," he asked.

"He would have arranged for her to go straight to a public place," Samaritan said. "There's probably a pay phone there that she's been instructed to wait near for secondary contact.''

''But New York is a big place,'' said Calderon. ''How do you know she's gone there?''

''I taught the son of a bitch everything he knows,'' Samaritan snapped. ''And at least I know there's no such thing as the New York City Zoo.'' Samaritan folded the map. ''Signal the unit. Let's go.''

There was a black government sedan standing by. As the men raced toward it, Samaritan took out his cell phone and keyed in a number, the direct line to Arthur Beller's private phone. The WITSEC head answered on the first ring.

''Beller here.''

''Sir? Samaritan.''

''Go ahead.''

''We have our mole,'' Samaritan said, with a slight smile.

The Central Park Zoo covered four or five acres near the southeast corner of the giant park in mid-Manhattan. Lee Cullen had been waiting nervously near the phone booth for nearly an hour, pacing and gnawing on her fingernails. She looked suspiciously at every person who passed by, but there was nothing remotely threatening about the mothers and children, or nannies and their charges who wandered around the zoo's precincts.

Lee almost jumped out of skin when the public address system crackled into life. "Your attention please. The zoo will be closing in ten minutes. . . ."

She looked down at her watch. Ten minutes to five. She looked around, praying she would see Eraser somewhere in the crowd. Instead, she felt a hand clasp her shoulder.

Lee whipped around. She had never seen this man before—and she would have remembered: He had an ugly J-shaped scar on his face. It was at odds with his neat, clean, almost preppy clothing and demeanor.

"Miss Cullen?"

Lee jammed her hand into her bag and squeezed the handle of the revolver. "Stay back!"

J-Scar smiled pleasantly, backing up slightly, his hands out, nonthreatening. Lee could see a glint of the gun in his belt.

"It's okay, ma'am," said J-Scar. "I'm here to help." He dug an I.D. card and a badge from the back pocket of his khakis. "United States Marshall, ma'am. I work with John Krueger."

Lee backed off a little, looking hesitant. "So where is he then? I was supposed to meet him here, not you."

"It's okay," said J-Scar. "John's on his way. He sent me here to keep you safe until he shows up."

"Really?" said Lee. "He said that might happen . . . I guess he would have told you about the secret handshake, right? The one you're supposed to give me so I know you're on the level."

This time J-Scar looked hesitant, but he managed to cover. "Yes," he said, "of course."

Lee thrust out her hand. "You don't mind if I check it out, do you? He told me I had to do it."

J-Scar took her hand. "No, that's fine. You can't be too security conscience. That's procedure—"

Lee grabbed his hand and yanked J-Scar into her and rammed her shoulder bag into his leg. She pulled the trigger of the revolver, blowing a hole in her leather bag and an even more jagged one in J-Scar's leg.

J-Scar screamed in pain and toppled to the pavement, clutching his leg, bright red blood pumping hot through his fingers. Lee was off and running before he fell, the thirty-eight in her hand.

**S**amaritan's black sedan squealed to a halt at a Fifth Avenue entrance to the park. The three men got out and strode toward the gate.

"Take her down if you have to," Samaritan

ordered. "But don't kill her. I want her alive. Got it?"

Calderon and Schiff nodded.

"Good. Get going."

The two spooks took off, pushing through the zoogoers, going against the traffic out of the zoo. Samaritan walked up to one of the zoo guards who was standing with two of Samaritan's New York agents.

"Close the gates," Samaritan commanded. "We have to make sure she's trapped inside."

"But there are still other people inside the zoo," said the security man. "We're not quite closed yet."

"The hell with that," Samaritan snapped. "Move them out! Now! My men will supervise."

It was getting dark and Lee turned it to her advantage, staying in the shadows and working her way toward the exit, trailing in the wake of the last few stragglers making their way out of the zoo. A few yards from the front gate, she saw that security guards and some men in dark suits were scrutinizing every person leaving the park. Lee knew trouble when she saw it. She stopped, turned, and ran back into the zoo.

Samaritan, Calderon, and Schiff were making their way through the zoo precincts, along with a number of the New York team. Lee saw them coming and darted behind a cage. Suddenly a family of six spider monkeys jumped up to the bars, screaming and shrieking, rattling the bars of the enclosure.

Startled, Lee jumped and ran again—but this time she was spotted by Calderon and Samaritan.

"There she goes!" Samaritan yelled. "Go get her." Calderon ran down the path. "Schiff, get over there and cut her off."

Lee raced through the petting zoo and by the large pond in the center of the park, scattering ducks and geese who quacked and honked indignantly as she ran right through the middle of the flock. The birds' angry noises tipped off Lee's pursuers, who came running—she had to find some cover and fast.

The park gates were up ahead, a cluster of security guards standing by the turnstiles. They saw the roaring, snorting truck bearing down on them and they quickly realized that whoever it was behind the wheel had no intention of stopping for a mere technicality like a gate.

Eraser blasted through the gates as if they weren't there, the smoking wreck of the truck screeching to a halt just inside the zoo. Eraser vaulted out of the truck, checking the Colt as he went, slapping a new, full clip into the handle.

Lee stood in the middle of the reptile house, staring at a living diorama of a jungle pond behind a forty-foot wall of glass, the waterline running halfway up the windowpane. Within the display huge crocodiles floated serenely, their elliptical eyes above the waterline, watching Lee. Beneath the water, she could see their awful, fang-studded jaws.

From the far end of the reptile house came the sound of breaking glass. Lee looked in horror and saw that one of Samaritan's killers was breaking the small glass window set in the middle of the door. As the thug reached in through the broken window to unbolt the door, Lee took off, running blindly, desperately searching for another way out of the building. She found a pair of double doors—the main entrance—but her heart sank when she tried the door handle. The door was firmly locked.

There were footsteps behind her—three men. Lee pressed herself into a shadowy corner and raised her gun, waiting until the three killers were close. Then she fired—the four shots sounding extremely loud in the space—blasting away until the gun clicked empty.

The silence following the burst of fire was deafening, but Lee could hear the men whispering in the darkness. She crouched down, as if trying to make herself as small as possible, trembling as the killers closed in. Just as the killers were about to close the trap, the double doors burst open and Eraser dove into the room, quickfiring his Colt. He grabbed Lee and hauled her behind a display case.

"You're late," said Lee.

"Sorry," said Eraser. "Traffic, you know."

Suddenly, bullets slammed into the display case, shattering it. Eraser saw that the bullets were coming from different angles—he and Lee were surrounded. He ejected the magazine from the Colt and checked the ammunition in the clip. There were only two rounds left. He peered into the darkness, then looked over at the smashed front doors, estimating the distance.

"You ready to get out of here?" Eraser whispered.

"I think I've seen enough," Lee replied.

"Then stay down," he hissed. "When I tell you to go, head for the door and run like hell."

As if given a command, all of the men opened fire at once, destroying the display case, exposing Eraser and Lee. Eraser pivoted and fired his last two rounds, blasting away—not at the killers, but at the window of the crocodile tank.

The glass shattered and tons of water exploded into the room, a tidal wave of green water knocking the killers off their feet. Four huge crocodiles were swept out of the tank, shooting through the break like logs down a chute. The fearsome reptiles hit the concrete floor in an ugly mood—

their bodies were stiff, their heads high, jaws locked wide open.

Eraser and Lee charged for the door, sloshing through ankle-deep water. One of the would-be killers charged after them, but he didn't move fast enough to outrun the twenty-foot croc that lunged for him. The jaws closed around his torso, ripping into his flesh, and the crocodile lifted him up, the hapless man kicking and screaming, firing his gun wildly. As if offended by the noise, a second croc reared up and crunched off his gun arm, tearing it away from the man's body.

Another killer had Eraser and Lee in his sights, but before he could fire, another crocodile burst out of the darkness and bit, snapping of his head, blood shooting into the air from his neck, as if from a fountain.

The gunfire stopped for a moment, then started up again—the doorway was full of Samaritan's men, blasting away wildly into the darkness. Eraser and Lee had no choice—their exit was blocked, so they had to double back toward the roar of the crocodiles and the screams of the dying killers echoing in the darkness.

Eraser and Lee splashed through the water, stopping only to grab a gun from the mangled corpse of one of the killers. As he turned, a five hundred pound crocodile—the biggest one in the reptile house—reared up out of the water, the razor-toothed jaws wide open, ready to strike. Eraser emptied the .45 right down the throat, the bullets blowing its reptilian brains out of the back of its skull.

"You're luggage!" Eraser said.

Calderon and Samaritan were at the door now, firing as fast as they could. Eraser grabbed Lee and crashed straight through a window, rolling out into the darkness as glass shards rained down around them.

Samaritan and Calderon started after them, but quickly scrambled back to safety when two crocodiles lunged for them, their tails thrashing.

"Christ!" Samaritan yelled. "Fucking crocodiles! Now I've seen everything."

# 13

The shoot-out at the Central Park Zoo was serious enough to require the presence of Arthur Beller himself—he was going to spend a lot of time calming down the mayor of New York and half a dozen law enforcement agencies, but first he wanted to get a look at the scene of the debacle.

A WITSEC helicopter landed Beller on the large expanse of lawn called the Sheep Meadow, not far from the Central Park Zoo. Samaritan met his chief, looking solemn and concerned.

"How many casualties?" Beller asked.

"Three men from the CIA," said Samaritan. "The ones you assigned to us. Krueger killed them, shot them like dogs."

Beller shook his head slowly. "I don't believe this. . . . He's our most dedicated operative. He's about as good as they come."

Samaritan did not react to this unspoken criticism of his own skills. "His prints are all over the murder weapon," he said.

Beller looked at him sharply. "You've run prints already? You're moving pretty fast there, officer."

"Krueger's not the only dedicated man you've got," Samaritan said acidly. Then he added, as if an afterthought: "Sir."

Beller was to immersed in thought to notice the sarcasm. "It doesn't make sense," he said. "Why would he do a thing like this? A career of exemplary service and then he goes off the rails."

"Well," said Samaritan, "the man's got no family, no friends, no real ties at all—he's got nothing to keep him honest. Nothing to lose, if you think about it. I think someone got to him. He's been bought."

"Christ . . . I've known John Krueger for years."

"We're losing time here, sir," said Samaritan impatiently. "If Krueger's innocent, you tell me why he's on the run?"

Beller was silent. He had no answer to the question, but he wished with all his soul that he did.

"All right," the WITSEC chief answered after a long pause. "What about the witness?"

"I have reason to believe she's in it with him," said Samaritan firmly. "She could have gotten away a dozen times."

Now Beller was really surprised. "What the hell? She's in with him? Come on, Samaritan . . ."

"Sir, when we approached her in the open—identified ourselves—she didn't ask questions, she just started shooting. She wounded one of my people. Where did she get a gun if he didn't give it to her?"

The full extent of the disaster was now beginning to dawn on Arthur Beller. "The media is going to eat us alive on this."

"Look, sir," said Samaritan, "make me pointman on this. I trained Krueger. No one knows him like I do."

Beller nodded. "Fine. Do it. He's yours. Do whatever it takes. Just *bring him in*. Understand?"

"I understand, sir," said Samaritan suppressing the desire to smirk. "I'll bring him in."

"Good. Now I have to go see the mayor of this fair city." Beller walked toward a waiting limousine, while Samaritan turned to a New York Police Department captain, the watch commander for the Central Park Precinct.

"Captain!" Samaritan shouted.

"Sir?"

"Put out an all-points bulletin, citywide," Samaritan ordered. "Get the state police in on it, too. I want this town to be locked up so tight it'll make his balls ache. Got it?"

"Got it." The watch commander turned away so Samaritan could not see the grimace on his face. Like most law enforcement officers, he disliked other cops, particularly when they came into his town, throwing their weight around.

Arthur Beller spent an extremely unpleasant hour and a half with the mayor of New York, the police commissioner, and some guy in the city administration who had something to do with preventing cruelty to animals. The guy was up in arms about the upset that had been done to the crocodiles. It seemed that they didn't like loud noises and, the guy pointed out with an absolutely straight face: "Human flesh is very bad for a crocodile's digestion."

It was with some relief that Beller got back to his helicopter and headed home to Washington, D.C. Somewhere over Pennsylvania the cellular phone in his pocket sounded.

"Beller, here."

"Captain?"

Beller recognized Eraser's voice instantly and he jumped slightly as if he had gotten an electric shock. "John! Where the hell are you? Samaritan is turning the city upside down looking for you."

"I know . . ."

He also knew the NYPD could look for him for weeks and never find him. Eraser and Lee were at the highest summit of a church, up in the belltower of Our Lady of the Seven Sorrows, an old Catholic church on East One Hundred and Second street, an area just a hair too far uptown to be washed by the rising tides of gentrification. From their perch in the belfry they could see the lights of Manhattan spread out before them far to the south. A low, constant roar, the immutable sound of a living city rose up to them, punctuated, at intervals, by the high-pitched counterpoints of wailing police sirens.

Eraser stood between two stone archangels, the Archangel Michael his avenging sword held high in the night sky and the Archangel Gabriel, his long trumpet at his lips announcing the joyful news of the Second Coming. Lee was huddled in the shelter of Gabriel. She looked tired and wan, worn out with the tension and shocked by the bloodshed.

"John?" said Beller urgently. "John, you have to come in. The longer you stay out, the worse it's going to be for you."

"Samaritan is the mole," Eraser replied.

"He's after my singer. He killed the others just to flush her out."

"Look, just come in," said Beller.

"I have to protect my witness," said Eraser firmly. "If I bring her in, she'll go down. Samaritan can't afford to leave her alive."

Beller was getting angry now. "Damn it, John! Don't you understand that you're the one putting her in danger? Keep up this nonsense and you'll both end up dead. Get it, John?"

"Samaritan has been bought," said Eraser. "It's not safe to bring her in. Not yet. Not until I've taken care of the threat."

"I've got five people dead and federal agents who make you as the shooter," said Beller. "That's the threat you should be worried about right now, John. Now goddamn it, I don't want to see you getting hurt. Come in and we'll sort this thing out face-to-face."

Eraser was silent for a long moment. He wished he could believe that Beller had the power to shield Lee, but he knew that Samaritan would run over anybody who tried to get in his way and that included the WITSEC chief.

"John . . . ?"

"I'll call you back."

"When?"

"When I have proof." Eraser broke the connection, flipped the phone closed and jammed it into his pocket.

"What did he say?" Lee asked.

Eraser shrugged. "It's gone too far," he said soberly. "We're on our own from here on out."

"What are we going to do?"

"We can't stay on the run forever," said Eraser. "We need some hard evidence. Something we can use to nail Samaritan."

Lee gazed out over the city. Behind every lighted window there was a person, a story, a set of joys or sorrows, people preoccupied with their own problems. And yet she knew that there was no one in the entire city facing as difficult a predicament as she was facing now.

"Are you all right?" Eraser asked.

"John," she said. "There's something I haven't told you." Lee dug into her tattered shoulder bag and pulled out the makeup case, popped it open and showed him the glistening golden computer disk.

"You kept a copy?" Eraser said.

Lee nodded. "I was supposed to get it to a friend of mine—a reporter on the *Washington Herald*."

"Claire Isaacs," Eraser said.

"How did you know about her?"

Eraser paused for a moment, preparing himself for the hard truth he was about to reveal to her.

"Lee . . . Claire Isaacs is dead. They killed her."

Lee's eyes widened. "No . . ."

"I'm sorry," Eraser said softly.

Lee felt herself go numb with shock, as if she had been hit hard, pounded by a freight train of emotion.

"But they couldn't have known about her," Lee whispered. "I didn't tell anyone about her." She was trembling now and her voice was weak and shaky.

"They tapped your phone," Eraser said. "And that tap took them to Claire Isaacs."

"Oh, my God . . . poor Claire," Lee said. She felt sick and lightheaded, suddenly more afraid than she had been before. Eraser reached for her, pulling her close and holding her tight, as if his strong arms could shield her from the horror. Lee's eyes filled with tears.

"I just wanted to cover myself," she said. "That's all I wanted to do. I didn't know who to trust." The tears overflowed and coursed down her cheeks. Her voice was tight. "Claire is dead because of me . . . I killed her. Now I'm going to get us killed as well."

Eraser took the disk from her and held it in the palm of his hand. "No," he said, "this may be the only thing that keeps us alive."

Lee shook her head. "I don't even know

what's on it,'' she said. ''How can you bank on this thing?''

''We have to find out what's on it,'' said Eraser.

''I've tried,'' said Lee. ''It's completely hackerproof. There's no way to run it outside the Cyrex building. It has to be run on the dedicated, in-house Cyrex mainframe computer system.''

''Then that's where we'll run it,'' said Eraser, as if this was the easiest thing in the world.

''John,'' she protested, ''Cyrex is like a fortress. We can't go back there. They would be expecting that.''

''I'd hate to disappoint them,'' said Eraser grimly.

A small man in a clerical collar and worn cassock appeared at the head of the steep staircase.

''The streets are clear,'' the priest said. ''The police have returned to the safety of their donut shops.''

Eraser smiled. ''Lee, I'd like you to meet an old friend of mine, Father Rodriguez.''

''Of course,'' said the priest, ''I wasn't always Father Rodriguez. You could say I was born again . . . with a little help from our friend here.''

''Some of his Colombian associates wanted to introduce him to God personally,'' said Eraser.

Lee glanced at the pectoral cross Father Rodriguez wore on his chest. "So the cross is just a part of a disguise. Something WITSEC dreamed up, right? Who would look for you here, in a church?"

Father Rodriguez shook his head. "No," he said softly, "I've been given a second chance at life. This time I'm using it to do God's work. Now, is there anything else I can do for you?"

"We need a car," said Eraser. "Just for a day or so."

"Done," said the priest. "It burns as much oil as it does gas, but it's yours."

The car Father Rodriguez provided turn out to be—to Eraser's surprise—a Mercedes Benz. It was a very old, very beat-up Mercedes, but it ran smoothly, though it did have a prodigious thirst for oil.

They drove out of Manhattan, creeping through the dark streets, stopping at each traffic light, obeying the speed limit, doing nothing to attract attention. It was late at night and the city had slowed down somewhat, but there were still people on the streets, cabs cruising, drunks spilling out of bars.

Once they were on the far side of the river, the scene changed completely. The freeway was deserted, the dark countryside, a windswept void. It was as if they were the last people on earth.

**14**

The sun had just risen, but the lights in the Jefferson Memorial still burned. Undersecretary of Defense Daniel Harper walked along the edge of the Tidal Basin, Samaritan and Cyrex security chief Morehart flanking him. Up on Fifteenth Street, parked in the shadow of the Bureau of Printing and Engraving, was the secretary's long black limousine, two plainclothes security operatives leaning against the hood, watching their boss.

"So, what are you going to do?" Harper asked. "How are you going to get us out of the mess you got us into?"

"I'll have the situation contained in twenty-four hours," said Samaritan smoothly. "Tops."

Harper shook his head. "That's just not good enough."

"Look," said Samaritan, "we have problems,

I know. But they can be solved. But first we have
to cancel that shipment.''

"You just don't get it, do you?'' Harper
snapped. ''The money has changed hands. These
are not the sort of people you cancel on. You get
those guns out of the country tonight or you are
a dead man. Understand?''

Samaritan was silent. He wasn't used to meet-
ing men more ruthless than he was. It was a very
unpleasant sensation.

"Now then,'' Harper continued, ''tell me how
you plan on containing this situation.''

"It's simple,'' said Samaritan. ''Krueger is on
the run, but he'll go to Cyrex. He has to. When
he shows, I'll be waiting.''

"Cyrex?'' said Morehart. ''Why the hell would
he risk going to Cyrex? That would be the last
place he would choose.''

"He's got the duplicate disk, right?'' Samaritan replied. ''He needs to know what's on it—
there's no other way to clear himself and the
woman. The disk can only be read in the Cyrex
mainframe, so he has to go there. Got it now?''

Harper did not look happy with this plan, but
he could see no alternative. ''Fine,'' he said.
''This better work. The disk . . . the girl . . . the
guns. By dawn the guns are out of the country,
and the disk and the girl eliminated. Clear?''

"Crystal,'' said Samaritan.

* * *

Just off Wisconsin Avenue, the main drag of the Georgetown section of Washington, D.C., was a bar—and it was the one place in the city that Eraser was sure he could get help he could trust. He and Lee stood in front of the place, Lee looking quite dubious.

"You sure about this?" she asked.

"I don't know where else to go," Eraser said. "There's no one else, not in Washington."

"Okay," she said with a shrug. "You're the boss. But I've never been to a gay bar before."

"You'll like it," Eraser said. "For once you won't get hit on."

"Yeah, but I bet you do."

It was a bright sunny day outside, but within the AC/DC Bar it could have been midnight. The lunch crowd was out in force, every table occupied by government workers, Washington staffers who were gay and didn't give a damn who knew it, though homosexual Department of Defense personnel were rarely seen here at any time of the day or night.

Behind the bar, looking hopelessly out of place, was none other than Johnny Casteleone, Johnny C, late of Royal Oak, Michigan. He glanced up when Lee and Eraser entered the dimly lit bar, focusing on Lee first—women were infrequent visitors to the AC/DC—then looking to her companion. He almost dropped the beer mug he was polishing when he caught sight of Eraser.

"Holy shit!" he said. "You!"

"Hi, Johnny," said Eraser. "This is Lee."

"Nice to meet you." He pulled them both a beer. "Okay, okay. . . I'm glad you're here," he said. "I've just got one question. Was it your idea to sign me up with the Village People here? It's been bugging the hell out of me."

"You're safe, aren't you?"

"From the mob, sure." Johnny C looked around the room. "But not from the ass pirates that come into this place."

"I'm sure you can take care of yourself." Eraser leaned in, his voice low. "You told me that if I ever needed anything I could come to you. Remember? That offer still good?"

Johnny C didn't hesitate. "What? You need my help? You got it." He stripped off his apron and threw it down on the bar.

"Hey, Kev," he called to the other bartender. "Cover for me, would ya? I got friends here who need a little help."

"Where are you going?" Kevin asked. His eyes ran over Eraser and he seemed to like what he saw. "Who's he?"

"Come on," Johnny C said with a groan,

"don't bust my chops. I hate it when you bust my chops."

Eraser couldn't help but laugh. "Maybe you two would like to be alone for a minute or two."

Johnny C shot Eraser an extremely dirty look. "We're fine, thank you. Kev, he's just a buddy. I'll be back."

Johnny C came out from behind the bar and headed for the exit, aware of Eraser's and Lee's curious, bemused glances. "Look, Kev's okay. It's just . . ."

"Yes?" said Eraser.

"It's just . . . you know, he worries about me."

"That's very nice," said Eraser.

"Get off it, would ya?"

Johnny C had taken some of the relocation money WITSEC had given him and invested it in a new, sky-blue Cadillac Coupe de Ville. The car was a little flashier, more noticeable than Eraser would have liked, but he was not in a position to be fussy about his ride.

Johnny drove. Eraser rode shotgun. Lee was in the back.

"So," said Johnny C, "where we going?"

"Virginia," said Eraser. "Crystal City."

"You got it."

Crystal City was just over the Virginia/District of Columbia line, a heavily developed suburb littered with tall, glass-plated skyscrapers, monuments to the corporations that did business with the United States government and got rich on federal largesse. In the middle of the forest of office buildings stood the glistening glass monolith that was the Cyrex Corporation's world headquarters.

"So what we do in Crystal City?" Johnny C asked when they made it to the congested suburb.

"We're going in there," said Eraser, pointing to the Cyrex building. "And we have to get in there quick."

Johnny C looked at Eraser, wondering if his rescuer had suddenly taken leave of his senses. "Are you shitting me? That's what you want my help for? I thought you needed a sofa moved or something." He half turned and glanced at Lee. "Is he on the level?"

"I'm afraid he's serious," said Lee. "I'm serious about it, too. We have to get inside that building."

"Well, I don't . . . ." said Johnny C petulantly.

"You said if I ever needed anything," Eraser said. "Make a left-hand turn up here."

Johnny C put the car into the turn. "Okay, okay. . . you want to break into the CIA, huh? Well, that's no problem. I figure all we're gonna need is a couple of tanks, a little air support, a couple of choppers, and a rocket launcher for each of us and, if you can get 'em, a division of marines. Then I figure we'll just stroll right in. Can you order up that stuff? 'Cause we're gonna need it.''

Eraser shook his head. ''Nope,'' he said. ''You don't need any of that stuff. All you need are these.'' He held up a couple of packets of Alka Seltzer.

''Ohhh,'' said Johnny C sarcastically, ''you didn't *tell* me you were packing antacids. Well, that changes everything.''

# 15

Night was falling and the forecourt in front of the Cyrex building was ringed with vans from the three television networks, CNN and half a dozen foreign-language stations. There were camera crews everywhere and correspondents stood in the glare of food spots, taping stand-ups for broadcast. Some technicians had set up the tall transponders on the broadcast vans, ready to do live remote telecasts for the network news shows later that night.

The nerve center of the Cyrex building that night was the security control room high up on the twenty-second floor. It was a windowless room, crammed with video equipment and screens mounted on the consoles, each staffed by a Cyrex operative. From this room almost every corner of the building could be monitored and patrolled.

Samaritan sat ensconced in the security center, watching the television coverage intently.

"The House Armed Services Committee has announced that two weeks from today it will begin official hearings into the Cyrex Corporation scandal," a female reporter said earnestly.

Samaritan chuckled. "And in two weeks from now I'm going to be lying on the beach of the island I plan to buy."

"Sources have revealed that the committee intends to peel the veil off the Pentagon's black budget," the reporter continued. "Finally, the weapons technology industry will be made accountable to the public for the first time. This news comes amid rumors of a key insider witness whose testimony is expected to lead to several federal indictments. . . ."

Samaritan wasn't smiling now. That Lee Cullen was still at large he took as a personal slight; that he had been outwitted by Eraser was a burning insult. He was going to make sure that he eradicated that black mark on his otherwise unblemished record—and he was going to do it that very night.

Morehart came up behind him and listened to the end of the television reporter's story. He took out a handkerchief and mopped his glistening brow. "This is a total nightmare," Morehart muttered. "The whole thing is going into melt down. There's no way out of this."

Samaritan was as cool as a tray of ice. "Bull-shit," he said. "You boys just do what I tell you and this time tomorrow you can all upgrade your memberships in those candy-ass country clubs you guys belong to."

Morehart looked skeptical. "I hope you're right about that," he said, stowing away his hand-kerchief. "Because if you're not—"

"So who's running this rumpus room any-way?" Samaritan asked.

"I am." A tall, broad-shouldered man stepped forward. He had a deeply lined face and huge hands, his posture was erect, his body language radiated absolute self-confidence—the kind of confidence that is part of the equipment they issue you for a long stretch as a Navy SEAL.

"You are, huh?" said Samaritan. "And who are you?"

"This is James Haggerty," said Morehart said quickly. "He's our head of security."

Samaritan and Haggerty appraised each other, each man taking the measure of the other. Nei-ther man seemed particularly impressed.

"The magic phrase here is low profile, Hag-gerty," Samaritan said. "Tell me, have you ever done any wetwork?"

"Only on three different continents," Haggerty said with a smirk.

"Hey," Samaritan snapped back. "You want to impress me, then do your fucking job, okay? How many of your people can we bring into this? I hope you have some good people here."

Haggerty bristled at Samaritan's dismissive tone of voice, but he managed to keep his temper in check.

"I've got eight," the big man said. "And they're all experienced professionals. They'll do whatever it takes to get the job done. There's another twenty on the security force."

Samaritan snorted. "Rent-a-cops? What good are they? Think they're gonna let themselves get shot for minimum wage?"

"They're more than that," Haggerty replied angrily. "They'll follow orders, but they're not part of the program."

"Okay," said Samaritan. "I believe you. . . . I've got three of my people downstairs at the main entrance to the building. Did you circulate Krueger's picture to all of your team?"

Haggerty nodded, pointing to the bank of surveillance television monitors on the console in front of them. "Yeah," he said, "I've got every possible point of entry under observation, from the roof top to the sewer system."

"That's nice," said Samaritan sarcastically,

"but don't count on that being enough. This fucker is a ghost. Believe me, if Krueger wants in, he'll get in. where does he have to go to run the disk?"

"He'll have to get to the central vault." Morehart pointed to another monitor. Two killers were stationed in front of the imposing vault doors. They were serious-looking guys dressed in black fatigues and tactical assault vests, the body armor festooned with grenades. "If John Krueger wants to read that disk, there's only one way. There's only one drive that can decode it."

"That's outstanding," said Samaritan. This time he sounded as if he meant it. "All we have to do is wait for Krueger to come to us."

But Haggerty wasn't paying attention. Rather, he was studying one of the monitors, the screen tracking the action in the lobby of the building.

"Hey, hey . . ." he said. "What have we got here?"

It was Johnny C. He pushed through the crowd of press and curious onlookers clustered at the door and strolled across the wide lobby as if he was out for an afternoon walk. He was carrying a pizza box.

"Gotta delivery here for Mr. Todross," said Johnny C to one of the uniformed guards. "He's up on the fourteenth floor."

"I'm sorry, pal," said the guard, "but I'm not allowed to accept any unauthorized deliveries."

"Oh," said Johnny C. "No problem. All you gotta do is call Todross on fourteen and have him authorize his extra cheese and pepperoni here."

"You can't just walk in here with a pizza, you know," the guard said crankily. "This is a high-security facility."

"And this is a Papa Genoche's pizza, my man," said Johnny C. "And if the customer doesn't get it while it's hot, then he gets two pizzas for free. And them two free pies come outta my pocket. *Capeesh?*"

Calderon led Hansen and Monroe, his new CIA associates over to Johnny C. Gently but firmly, they took hold of him. Johnny C wrenched himself out of their grasp, shrugging off their hands.

"Hey!" he said. "What the hell are you doing?"

"Would you step over here, please," said Calderon.

Hansen grabbed the pizza from Johnny C's hands, while Calderon and Monroe slammed him up against the wall.

"Easy!" yelped Johnny C. "I got a heart condition and a really good lawyer, you know—"

"Shut up," Calderon ordered, roughly patting him down. The press outside had begun to notice the commotion. Cameras were being pointed in Johnny C's direction.

As the flashbulbs began to pop, Johnny C doubled over, surreptitiously slipping the Alka Seltzer tablets into his mouth. He clutched at his heart and stared at Calderon, wide-eyed, foam starting from his mouth. Johnny C then kicked it up a notch, flipping into a convincing grand mal seizure.

Suddenly, Calderon heard Samaritan's voice crackling in his ear piece. "What the fuck is going on down there?"

He whipped his walkie-talkie off his belt and keyed it. "Some civilian is going into a seizure, sir."

Haggerty was staring at Johnny C's image on the monitor. "Is that the man we're waiting for?"

Samaritan chuckled and shook his head. "No, that's not him. When Krueger comes, he won't try any cornball delivery trick, you can bet on that. So, which one of you geniuses ordered a pizza?"

Morehart watched the monitor, growing more apprehensive as the media attention increased.

"This is all we need!" he said unhappily. "Haggerty, get him to the infirmary immediately and call an ambulance. And make sure he stays clear of the goddamned press. Understand?"

"Right," said Haggerty, reaching for a phone.

\* \* \*

Calderon and the rest of his team gathered around Johnny C. He was on the floor, foaming at the mouth, convulsing like a tuna that had just been clobbered with a fisherman's gaffe.

A beefy Cyrex nurse and her burly assistant rushed through the security checkpoints at the back of the lobby, trundling a gurney. "Okay," the nurse ordered. "Back up, everybody, let's give him some air."

Johnny C snuck a look at the two medical technicians. It struck him that even the Cyrex nurses looked tough.

Samaritan kept one eye on the monitor, while he dialed a number with his cell phone. He watched as the nurse and the orderly slung the still foaming Johnny C onto the gurney, strapping him down securely.

The phone rang in the Cyrex warehouse in Staunton, Virginia, and as Samaritan waited for an answer, he saw the gurney being wheeled away.

Schiff answered on the third ring.

"It's Samaritan. How're we doing?"

Schiff looked out to the warehouse floor. The place was vast and as immaculate as a laboratory and was full of white-jacketed technicians who were loading crated rail guns into two forty-foot sea containers.

"The trucks should be out of here before midnight," Schiff reported. "Right on time."

"Good," said Samaritan with a nod. "They need to roll or I need to know why, okay, Schiff?"

"Yeah, yeah," said Schiff wearily. He was looking forward to the day when he would no longer have to take orders from Samaritan.

The nurse and the attendant rushed Johnny C into the infirmary in the rear of the Cyrex facility.

"Try to stay calm," said the nurse. "Help is on the way. We'll have you in a hospital in no time."

Johnny C wasn't all that worried about his physical condition. What was bothering him was that he was running out of foam. A minute or two more and his serious condition would have miraculously cleared up.

The gurney blew through the double swinging doors of the sick bay and stopped suddenly. As the orderly pasted a heart sensor to his chest, the nurse slipped on a stethoscope and listened to Johnny C's heart. As Johnny tried to fake one more foamy convulsion, he ripped the wire from the hot monitor, which flat lined instantly, generating a high-pitched beep.

"Oh, my God!" said the nurse, tearing the

stethoscope from her ears. "He's fibrillating! We've got code blue!"

She jammed a thick galvanized rubber bit between his teeth, Johnny C's eyes going wide as it dawned on him what was about to happen. The attendant was rolling over the cardiac shock cart, rubbing the paddles together to spread the conductor gel on the electrodes.

The nurse grabbed the paddles and pushed them against the bare skin over Johnny C's heart. He was wailing behind the rubber bit and shaking his head frantically from side to side, but his frenetic spasms seemed to be just more evidence that he was one sick puppy.

"Clear!" the nurse shouted.

The attendant stepped away as the nurse let Johnny C have it, two hundred volts blasting through his body. He arched with the shock, convulsing again, but for real this time.

The ambulance arrived at the rear of the Cyrex building, sirens wailing, lights flashing. At the wheel was Eraser dressed in the orange jumpsuit of a District of Columbia EMS technician. Next to him was Lee, dressed in the same uniform.

The guard at the loading dock hardly looked at them. "They've been waiting, come on!"

The guard ushered them through the back door, toward a metal detector. Eraser stepped through, handing his medical bag to the guard, who opened it and glanced in and handed it back. The folding gurney that Lee was pushing set off the alarm as it passed through the arch of the metal detector.

The guards ignored the alarm. Instead, they hurried Eraser and Lee down the long corridor.

"Let's move it!" the guard yelled. "Go! Go! Go!"

Up in the security control room, Samaritan glanced at the monitor with little curiosity. As far as he was concerned, they were just two EMS techs pushing a gurney. Doing their job.

In the infirmary, Johnny C, dazed and quivering was about to get another jolt of life-giving electricity. The nurse was confused. The heart monitor was still beeping, the green line on the scope was still flat, but Johnny C was obviously not only alive, but still conscious.

"Okay," she said. "Let's do it again."

The infirmary doors flew open as Eraser pushed the gurney through the double doors, Lee right behind him.

"Let's not . . ." Eraser reached under the cart and tore away a 9mm Glock taped to the underside. He pointed it at the guard, the nurse, and the attendant. Lee unbuckled the belts that bound Johnny C to the gurney.

"Oh, my God!" the nurse gasped. "Terrorists!'' She knew Cyrex was on high alert—now she knew the reason why.

Johnny C, still gasping, grabbed the gun from the guard's holster. ''Terrorists?'' he snarled. ''You want terror, lady? I'll give you terror! Tell you what we should do, I think we should lie you down and strap your ass to the shock machine there and jump start you!''

The nurse looked as if she was going to faint. ''Please,'' she said, her voice hoarse, ''please don't hurt me.''

Johnny C looked slightly embarrassed. ''Oh, come on . . . I wouldn't hurt a nurse. What kind of animal do you think I am?''

Eraser stepped up. ''You three, on the floor,'' he said. ''I want you to face the wall. Now.''

The guard, the nurse, and the orderly did as they were told. Eraser tossed a roll of duct tape to Johnny C.

''Tape them up, Johnny,'' Eraser ordered. ''And keep the room secure. Get the keys.''

Lee knelt down and snatched a key ring from the security guard's belt. ''Got 'em,'' she said.

''Okay,'' said Eraser, ''let's move.''

# 16

Samaritan sipped a Diet Pepsi and waited—he had been waiting a long time and he was beginning to wonder if he had misjudged John Krueger. Had he backed out of the challenge? Would he come or was Cyrex just too tough a nut to crack? He had never known Krueger to back down—his refusal to go down on the WITSEC jet was just the latest in a long series of dangerous situations in which Eraser had refused to bow to wisdom and give up.

Samaritan took another swig of soda. No, John Krueger would be checking in some time tonight. He could feel it in his bones.

Suddenly the computer screens on the security-center consoles began flashing a series of numbers in rapid sequence, information slotting up on the screen with ever increasing speed.

A technician whipped around on his rolling

chair and rapidly punched in a series of commands on his keyboard. "Jesus Christ," he muttered. "The whole system is going nuts. . . ."

"What? What?" Samaritan demanded. "What's happening?"

Morehart and Haggerty gaped, as information scrolled down the screens.

"I think I know what this means," said Morehart.

"What?" Samaritan said, bolting upright. "What's happening?"

"He's running the disk," said Morehart. "I can't believe it. He's running the goddamned disk. Right here in the building!"

"Impossible," said Haggerty. He keyed up the screen showing the entrance to the computer vault. The burly guards in the body armor were still standing there, alert and on duty. Haggerty picked up his walkie-talkie. "Station One. Any activity at your location?"

"Negative," said one of the guards into his own hand transmitter. "All clear here."

Haggerty turned around and looked straight at Samaritan. "It's some kind of glitch. It's gotta be. There's no way—"

Samaritan shook his head derisively. "Glitch my ass. He's in there all right. He just didn't use the door, that's all. Haggerty, get your team down there—and I mean get them down there now!"

Samaritan strode toward the door, Haggerty and Morehart following him. They picked up a squad of Haggerty's operatives as they made their way down to the vault room. Every one of the men was heavily armed, jacking rounds into the chambers of their weapons, ready to launch the assault.

Samaritan stopped in front of the heavy vault door. "Okay, open it up, Mr. Morehart."

Morehart stepped forward and punched the numerical password into the keypad mounted on the wall next to the vault door. The door remained shut. Morehart hesitated a moment, then entered the number again, but the door did not open.

"What?" said Samaritan angrily. "What are you doing? Why can't you get this damn thing open?"

Morehart nervously pushed his glasses back up his nose. "Look, I know this. We change the password once a week, but I know this." Morehart's finger was poised above the buttons, but he didn't press any buttons, unsure of what to do next. He swallowed hard.

"Oh, the hell with that," said Samaritan, shoving Morehart to one side. He grabbed a shotgun—a nice big one—from one of the armed men, racked it and jammed the muzzle up against the locking mechanism of the vault door. He pulled both triggers and blew the keypad off the wall, shattering it. The locks on the door hesitated a moment, then disengaged, the vault doors rolling back silently. The hit team swarmed into the small room, weapons raised, ready for a firefight in the confined space. But the vault was empty.

While the hardcases gaped, Samaritan pushed through them and looked around. He did not look happy. The huge computer was running, the screens flashing data at incredibly high speed as the program downloaded. Samaritan turned on Morehart, his eyes blazing.

"Okay," he said, "talk to me. And talk fast."

"I don't know . . . I . . . I . . ." Morehart looked stunned, as if he had been punched hard in the face.

Samaritan grabbed him by the lapels of his expensive suit and got up in his face. "I said, talk to me. He's here. So where is he?"

"He must be running the program from a remote terminal," said Morehart. "That's all it can be."

"Remote? Where?"

"Somewhere in the building," said Morehart. "It can't be outside. The whole system is dedicated to operate within the walls of this building. I can't believe this is happening."

"Well, it is happening," said Samaritan angrily. "And I thought you told me it could only be run from this location."

"He can't," said Morehart miserably. "Donahue designed this system specifically so that no outside access would be possible, ever."

Samaritan pulled his pistol from his shoulder holster and jammed it under Morehart's chin.

"Donahue's dead," Samaritan said through clenched teeth. "And you're going to wish you were, too, Morehart. Unless, that is, you find out what the fuck is going on and you find out now!"

Morehart started to shrivel, whimpering, sure that he was about to be shot to death. But Haggerty stepped up. He was red in the face and he looked very angry. He grabbed Samaritan by the shoulder and tried to pull him away from the hapless and very scared Morehart.

"Holster your weapon," Haggerty ordered.

Samaritan didn't even look at him. "Listen, why don't you take a walk around the block, junior?"

Haggerty put a little more pressure on Samaritan's shoulder—and that was a mistake. Samaritan moved so fast, he was a blur. It took about a second to whip Haggerty around, slamming his head onto the console of the computer workstation, his arm twisted up behind his back, the muzzle of Samaritan's gun jammed into the back of Haggerty's head.

"Some people take a lot for granted," Samaritan said. "Like the ability to chew food."

"I think we can find him," Morehart said timidly.

As Samaritan turned to Morehart, he let Haggerty fall to the floor. The big man was out cold.

"What?" he asked. "What did you say?"

"I think we can find him," Morehart repeated. "We can get the computer technicians to scan every terminal in the building. Go through the workstations, eliminate them one by one. If he stays on line, he can be nailed."

"Then get going. Do it," said Samaritan quickly. "But just make sure you do it fast. . . ."

Eraser and Lee were huddled over a computer, but not one in the secure vault of the Cyrex building. Rather, they were in the office that had once been occupied by Cyrex CEO William Donahue. The curtains were wide open, but there was a piece of plywood covering the window shattered by the bullet Donahue had fired into his own brain. The only sound was the rapid click of computer keys as Lee's fingers danced across the keyboard. On the screen there was one large display bearing the heading: AEP TOR SCHED—

and followed by a long list of scrambled and encoded words.

"You were right," said Lee. "I never would have guessed that Bill Donahue would have circumvented his own computer system. Security was his one great obsession. This dedicated system was his invention."

"Scum like Donahue always leave themselves a back door," said Eraser. "It makes them feel powerful, like they're above the common herd." He glanced at his watch. "I figure we've got five, maybe six minutes before they trace our signal. You recognize that code?"

Lee shook her head," No, but we're getting warm," she said. "I know it's an accounting format. That's a step in the right direction."

"Right," said Eraser. "Stop me if I get lucky."

Samaritan and Morehart leaned over the shoulders of the computer technician as he raced through the programs governing the Cyrex computer network. A graphic popped up on the screen washing out an entire wing of the building.

"The south wing is clean," the techie announced. "I'm going to do a slave and driver check of the rest of the building. Two more to go." The keyboard rattled under his fingers like hailstones on a window.

Samaritan pulled Calderon in close. "This

whole piss-poor event is going to be over in ten minutes,'' he whispered. ''I want a chopper on the roof, now. Gassed and waiting.''

Calderon nodded. ''You got it.''

Sheets of information, numbers and words, washed across the computer terminal in Donahue's office. Lee studied them closely.

''I know those codes,'' she said. ''Those are offshore banking deposits. UBS—that's Union Banc Suisse.'' She clicked into the file and together they looked over the data.

''Fifty-two million dollars,'' said Eraser, ''If that figure represents an arms' sale, then it's a major one. Let's see who the buyer is.''

Lee entered the identify command. The screen went blank for a moment, but the running light blinked rapid. Suddenly pixels rained rapidly down the screen, quickly forming themselves into a black-and-white photograph which grew more distinct every few seconds.

It was the face of man, flat and washed out, an unflattering photograph, probably taken from an official document like a passport, driver's license, or security pass. His name slotted up under the picture.

''Sergei Ivanovich Petrofsky,'' Lee read. She looked to Eraser. ''That name mean anything to you?''

Eraser nodded slowly. "Yeah . . . he heads a cartel in the Russian Mafia. He'll sell anything he can get his hands on—guns, drugs, women, radioactive material that suddenly went missing from Russian government facilities. One thing for sure, whatever he sells, he always makes sure he sells it to some very unpleasant people. The more crooked the better."

"Yeah?" asked Lee. "But what's a guy like him doing with an international high-tech weapons deal?"

The answer was obvious to Eraser. "He's taking his cartel global. You need firepower for something like that. Those Russian gangs don't play any other game than hardball."

More data streamed on to the screen. "There's an end user's certificate dated for tomorrow morning at oh-four-thirty," said Eraser, his eyes locked on the screen. "End user is an official permit to export weapons—"

"I know that," Lee said quickly. "There was a time when I used to work in this business, remember?"

"Sorry, forgot. A thousand units for delivery at Baltimore harbor. Tomorrow, right before dawn."

"Yeah?" said Lee. "But a thousand units of what? Cyrex makes hundreds of different products."

"It can only be one thing," Eraser said. He leaned over Lee and punched the keys that would take him into a file called Product Information. The computer immediately shot back the required data.

It was a rotating computer graphic of a rail gun, complete with an X-scope. A sidebar ran down the right side of the screen giving dimensions and statistics along with the official name of the weapon.

EM-1 LIGHT RAIL ASSAULT SYSTEM

Lee stared at the images on the screen, stunned that the company that had employed her for so long could be involved in traffic so treacherous. She felt sick to her stomach.

"A goddamned electromagnetic gun," Lee said softly. "I don't believe it. They couldn't—"

"They could," said Eraser flatly. "Bet on it. The trouble is it's a thousand goddamn EM guns."

"Are they insane?" Lee asked. "They can't export these things. If they get offshore . . ."

"Petrofsky would become the godfather for terrorism in the twenty-first century," said Eraser soberly.

The enormity of the deal that was about to go down struck them hard. Eraser attacked the keys of the computer. "We need the name of that ship. And we need it now!"

* * *

"He's somewhere in the north wing," said Morehart's chief technician. "But there are fifteen
terminals running secure programs up there."

"Close enough," said Samaritan. "Calderon,
let's get moving." He slammed a walkie-talkie
down on the computer console next to the technician. "Keep hunting," he said. "When you nail
him, call me."

The hitmen swarmed through the long corridors
of the north wing of the Cyrex building, crashing
into offices, weapons drawn. Most offices were
empty; a few contained bewildered-looking office
workers who were putting in a little overtime,
trying to look like they were go-getters.

Suddenly, the computer operator's voice
blasted into Samaritan's ear. "I got him! Executive floor. They're in Donahue's office!"

"Great!" Samaritan shouted. "We're on our
way. Can you erase the disk he's working from?"

"Sure," the technician said. "I can wipe him
out as long as they stay locked in interface."

"Then do it now," Samaritan commanded.
"And I want you to send him a message."

Eraser and Lee were waiting for the name of the
ship to come up, the adrenaline pumping through
them. However, just as the name of the vessel

tied up in Baltimore harbor started to appear on the screen, the information vanished, erasing line by line. Both of them blinked.

"What's happening?" said Lee as the data disappeared right in front of their eyes. "What does this mean?"

"It means they're on to us," Eraser said grimly. "It means we have to get the hell out of here."

Eraser hit the eject button, trying to retrieve the disk in the A drive, but the cartridge did not boot out. He jammed his fingers into the drive and tried to pull it out, but the disk was locked solid. He grabbed a paper weight from the desk and smashed it into the plastic front of the machine, but the entire screen froze, then went blank.

There was a moment of blackness, then five block-letter words came up on the screen: YOU HAVE JUST BEEN ERASED. . . .

**17**

**B**arely a second after the contemptuous message appeared on the computer screen, the door of Donahue's office flew open and two of Haggerty's killers crashed into the room, guns up and ready.

The first man through the door got the full weight of Donahue's heavy desk chair, right in the neck. The man behind him was firing wildly, bullets peppering the room. Eraser dove for him and jammed his Glock into the man's belly and fired, backing him into the corridor.

"Lee! Go!" he said, rolling the corpse of the killer toward the elevator. "I'm right behind you."

The elevator chime sounded and the light above the door lit up. The doors swept open, the cab of the elevator containing three more SWAT-suited gunmen, each one of them armed for war.

Eraser shoved the dead killer at them, pulling the pin on one of the grenades attached to the dead man's body webbing. The doors rolled closed, and a second later, a muffled explosion echoed up the elevator shaft, the doors buckling outward from the force of the explosion.

The elaborate security system hardwired into the Cyrex building detected the explosion in an instant. Buzzers sounded, as Lexan screens started to descend from the ceiling, isolating the executive floor, locking it down.

Eraser raced down the hall, following Lee. But suddenly, a Lexan screen dropped between them.

"Run!" Eraser shouted. "I'll meet you at the ambulance."

Lee hesitated a moment, unsure of what to do.

"I said run," Eraser roared. "You can't do anything here."

Lee nodded and raced down the hall—straight into the arms of Samaritan. Lee struggled to get free, but he held her tight, a gun at her temple.

"Hey, Johnny," said Samaritan cackling, "look what I found here."

Eraser and Samaritan raised their weapons simultaneously and blasted away, rapid firing as if on a shooting range. The Lexan screen between them jumped and rattled as the bullets struck and bounced off. Eraser and Samaritan glared at each other, both enraged by the stalemate.

Samaritan tightened his grip on Lee. "Okay, Johnny," he shouted through the plastic shield. "Listen up. We finish this by my rules. You fuck with me in any way, I'll slice her up and mail the pieces back to you."

Lee struggled against his grasp, but she couldn't break free. Samaritan smacked the side of her head with the barrel of his pistol. Lee sagged in his arms, her hair against his cheek.

"Hey, John, guess what?" Samaritan smiled an evil smile. "Her hair smells like cinnamon, too. See ya."

Eraser watched helplessly as Samaritan dragged Lee's limp body into a stairwell. Eraser was trapped, boxed in by Lexan screens. There was only one way out that he could see. He raised his gun and blasted three sprinkler heads out of the ceiling. The sprinklers kicked in, drenching the corridor, the security alarm changing to a more urgent fire alarm.

A recorded announcement blared from half a dozen hidden loudspeakers. "This is not a drill, this is a fire warning. Please evacuate the area immediately. This is not a drill, this is a fire warning. . . ."

The screens started to lift. Eraser dove under one and charged for the stairwell, taking the concrete steps two at a time, racing for the roof. He burst through the door just as the chopper was lifting off the helipad. Samaritan and Lee were in the passenger compartment in the rear of the helicopter, Calderon and Monroe jammed together up front with the pilot.

Eraser and Samaritan locked eyes. Then Samaritan smiled and waved, mouthing the words "bye-bye" as the chopper rose in the sky. Eraser raised his weapon, but there was no clear shot.

Suddenly, one of the gunmen burst from the access door, blasting away with a fistful of handgun. Eraser ducked, rolled, and fired three times, dropping the killer in an instant. He looked back toward the chopper, but now it was nothing more than a small dot racing across the sky.

The elevator doors in the lobby swept open, police officers jumping back as Eraser emerged, the dead gunman from the roof cradled in his arms. As far as the police were concerned, Eraser was an EMS worker doing the job he was trained to do.

"Hey!" yelled one of the cops. "What the hell is going on here?"

"There's a data clerk upstairs!" said Eraser. "He's gone postal!" Eraser muscled by them as the cops piled into the elevator.

* * *

Johnny C was pacing the infirmary, agitated and worried. All over the building alarms were blaring and he had no idea what was going on. It was only a matter of time before someone entered the sick bay and saw the three prisoners bound and gagged on the linoleum floor.

Suddenly, Eraser burst through the open door, striding into the room, the dead gunman still in his arms.

"Who's that?" asked Johnny C.

Eraser slammed the body onto the gurney and jammed the needle of a rolling IV rig into the dead man's arm. "That's our patient."

Johnny C peered at the corpse. "I don't think he's gonna make it. . . ." He glanced around the room. "Where's Lee?"

Eraser's face was grim. "I lost her. Come on." They grabbed the gurney and bolted out of the infirmary. The scene on the loading dock was chaotic, employees running from the building as the alarm continued to blare. Eraser and Johnny C pushed the gurney straight down the ramp and over to the ambulance. They dumped the dead man in the back of the vehicle, climbed into the cab, and roared off. No one looked at them twice.

# 18

They dumped the ambulance and the stiff on a back street, then ran back to Johnny C's Cadillac.

"I can get us to Baltimore in forty minutes," said Johnny C. "I know all the shortcuts." He fired up the big engine and gunned it.

"Johnny," Eraser said, "look—"

"My Uncle Tony runs the docks in Baltimore," said Johnny C happily. He was glad to be out of Cyrex and on to more familiar territory, the grimy back streets of the Baltimore waterfront.

"Johnny," said Eraser, "you're not coming."

Johnny C laughed. "Oh, man, don't start with this James Bond 'I work alone,' shit. Please. This is me you're talking to."

"It's not your fight," said Eraser. "And it's going to get hot."

"Good," said Johnny C. "The hotter the better. I could use some action. You know how boring it is being a bartender in a gay bar? They don't get into fights or nothing," Johnny laughed. "And besides, what do you mean it's not my fight? What are you talking about? If it weren't for you, my tongue would stuffed and hung on Leo Canelli's trophy wall like some freakin' prize trout."

Eraser sighed. "Okay. Let's go."

"Great," said Johnny. He jammed the car into the gear and took off. "You'll like my cousin Tony. He's made his bones already and he and the harbormaster are thick as a brick. If your ship is there, he'll find it."

Johnny C's cousin, Tony Two Toes, was an extremely dangerous man, an ice pick in a four-thousand-dollar suit. He sat behind his beat-up old desk in his warehouse headquarters doing the thing he enjoyed most—counting money. Little Mike, Tony Two Toe's bag man had brought in that week's take from a very profitable loan-sharking operation that was Tony's main source of income. In the background, a sawed-off little killer known only as Sal was bent over a pool table, carefully setting up his shots. Sal was Tony's driver and bodyguard.

Tony worked through a pile of envelopes

stuffed with cash, working an adding machine fast, his fingers a blur. Suddenly, he stopped and stared at the tape on the calculator.

"Hey! Little Mike! You're an envelope short here. What kinda bullshit is that?" Tony Two Toes sounded more amazed than angry. No one had ever shorted him a payment before.

Little Mike shrugged. "Infantino didn't pay."

"He what!" Tony shouted. "Whaddya mean he didn't pay? What did he tell you?"

Little Mike opened his mouth to speak, but someone else answered for him. "He said tell that fat fuck Tony Two Toes I ain't gonna pay him another dime and he don't like it, he can kiss my bony Sicilian ass."

Little Mike, Sal, and Tony jumped, then looked to see two figures silhouetted in the doorway.

"I know the voice," said Tony slowly. "But it can't be him. Not unless he's a ghost."

Johnny C stepped into the light. "Boo," he said, grinning from ear to ear.

"I don't believe this," said Sal. "Johnny C. I thought you got yourself good and whacked."

"Yeah," said Johnny C with a shrug. "I heard that, too. It musta been some other guy."

Tony Two Toes looked at his nephew, his eyes ice cold. "Yeah?" he said. "Was it some other guy who ratted out Leo Canelli?"

"Hey," said Johnny C. "Screw Canelli."

"I got no love for him either," said Tony Two Toes. "But you crossed the line, Johnny. What you did was wrong."

"What he did," said Eraser evenly, "was get a drug dealer and his poison off the streets."

"Johnny," said Tony, "I been meaning to ask you—who's this tree trunk you got here?"

"He's a friend," said Johnny C. "This is the guy who saved my ass not once but twice."

"Your funeral was absolutely beautiful, man," said Little Mike. "You shoulda been there."

"Really? Thanks, Mikey," Johnny replied. "Sorry I missed it."

"Next time," said Little Mike.

"Hey, Mr. Tree Trunk," said Tony. "I appreciate that you saved my nephew's life, but you should tell him that coming around here is not a very wise thing. If Canelli finds out he's still breathing . . ."

"Like I said, screw Canelli. We got bigger problems." He turned to Eraser. "Fill 'em in."

"There's a major weapons deal going down," said Eraser. "A U.S. contractor is selling out to international terrorists."

The three gangsters exchanged glances and chuckled. "Yeah? So? Who gives a shit about that?" said Tony. "Why should I interfere with some man just trying to make a living?"

"You should give a shit about it," said Eraser. "It's happening right here on your docks."

Tony looked to Little Mike and Sal again—there was no laughter this time. Horning in on a don's territory was a serious crime in their world.

"This is real high-tech Flash Gordon shit," said Johnny C. "This stuff'll fry your nuts off from a mile away. Buncha antiAmerican sons of bitches are trying to get their hands on 'em."

"These are the most dangerous assault weapons ever built," Eraser said solemnly. "They're called electromagnetic pulse rifles. We need your help. These men have to be stopped."

"This is on the level?" Tony asked.

Eraser nodded. "Yep. And they're holding an innocent woman hostage. If the ship sails . . . she dies."

There was a moment of silence as the facts sunk in.

"You know," said Tony. "There's a Russian registry in the harbor tonight." He snatched a clipboard off the wall and handed it to Eraser.

"The *Pobyeda* . . . a freighter."

Tony nodded. "Yeah, and it's a big one. It's berthed in Dock fifty-seven. That's a real quiet part of the harbor."

"Hey, Tony," Johnny C called out. "You packing any heat here?"

Tony Two Toes wagged a fat finger at his

nephew. "Now Johnny, you know that's illegal. You listen to me, both of youse . . . these are my docks, understand. And nobody is gonna go shooting them up, *capeesh?*"

"Aww, Tony," Johnny said. "Come on . . ."

"No one's shooting up my docks . . . unless I'm with 'em." He swept the envelopes off his desk and popped open a false top to reveal a dozen gleaming weapons, including a vicious little shotgun with a folding stock.

"Here," he said. "Take your pick."

As Eraser followed Tony onto the docks, he pulled his cellular phone from his pocket and hit the autodial connecting him with the WITSEC offices just a few miles away in Washington, D.C.

"It's Krueger," said Eraser. "Get me Beller."

Beller picked up immediately. "John? Where are you?"

Eraser ignored the question. "Cyrex is selling weapons to the wrong people. Daniel Harper is in it with them."

"Undersecretary of Defense Harper?" Beller asked. "Come on, John, this story of yours just keeps on getting stranger."

"It's the truth," said Eraser. "Samaritan is the facilitator. It all goes down tonight."

"John," Beller pleaded, "give yourself up and

we'll talk about it. Please, John, you're going to get yourself killed."

"Come and get me," he said. "Baltimore docks. Pier fifty-seven." That was all he had to say. Eraser didn't bother to hang up; he just tossed the cell phone into an open Dumpster and kept on walking, Beller's voice calling after him. As he went, he folded the stock of his little shotgun and chambered a round.

# 19

The container carrier *Pobyeda* was a forty-six-thousand-ton behemoth of a ship, the largest freight carrier in the Russian merchant marine fleet. But the large vessel was carrying no cargo—except for the three containers that were about to be loaded on board. A dozen Russian Mafia goons lounged around on deck, chain smoking Marlboros and jabbering away about what they would buy with their cut of the arms' profits.

As a crane hefted the first container off the dock, Sergei, the leader of the Russian pack went to the wardroom to pour himself a cup of coffee, watching as the container was raised high in the air.

Samaritan walked in, checking the clip in his gun.

"Expecting trouble?" Sergei asked. He sipped the steaming coffee and smacked his lips.

"I'm a boy scout," Samaritan answered coolly. "Always be prepared. That's my motto."

"Is that why you brought her?"

Lee Cullen was in a corner of the room, her wrists lashed to a chair with baling wire. She gazed at Samaritan with hatred in her eyes.

"Think of her as an insurance policy," Samaritan said. "Just in case someone decides to crash our little party here."

Lee strained against the wire that bound her wrists, the cable cutting into her flesh as she tried to work herself free.

Samaritan strapped on a Kevlar vest. "As soon as you're in international waters, her policy expires."

"And then?" asked Sergei.

Samaritan shrugged. "Do whatever you like," he said. "Personally, I'd bust a cap in her ass and toss her over the side."

Sergei walked over to Lee, his eyes traveling down her body. "You probably would, too. That would be such a waste."

Tenderly, he brushed her cheek with his thick fingers. Lee's skin felt like silk. She whipped her head away defiantly.

"Don't even think about it," she snapped.

Sergei smiled thinly, then hauled off and

cracked her across the face. He bent down and hissed in her ear. "I think what I like," said Sergei, "and I do what I like. You will soon learn this."

"The next crate is coming up," said Samaritan. "I'll leave you two lovebirds alone."

Samaritan had a mobile command van parked down on the dock in the shadow of the *Pobyeda*. He lowered himself into the seat in front of the console and grabbed a headset-microphone rig and put it on. He scanned the screens showing pale black-and-white views of various parts of the docks.

"Okay," he said into the microphone. "EM team report."

"Check." Schiff was positioned on the roof of an old, rusting warehouse near the ship.

"Check." Calderon was standing on a sea container tucked into the corner of a dock.

"Check." J-Scar was three stories above the dock, perched in the control cabin of the crane.

All three men were armed with rail guns fitted with the X-scopes.

"Okay," said Samaritan. "We're almost done here. So let's keep our eyes open, okay?"

**E**raser vaulted the boundary fence that surrounded the docks and made his way through the deserted container terminal, while Tony Two

Toes led his little band up to the main gate of the compound.

One of Samaritan's perimeter guards stopped them. "Let's hold it right there, guys," he said. "Docks are closed to outsiders."

"Outsiders?" said Tony indignantly. "I'm the president of the fuckin' union local. International Brotherhood of Longshoremen. We gotta a report you're using scab labor down here."

"I'm afraid I can't discuss that—"

"I didn't come here to discuss anything with you, pal," said Tony. "You got black-leg labor in there and we're gonna go down there and discuss it with them while kicking their scab asses. Got it?"

"Sir," said the guard, "this is a matter of national security. Leave the area immediately . . . or you will be detained."

Johnny C and Tony exchanged glances. Little Mike chuckled.

"Hey," Johnny C asked the guard, "you wouldn't be threatening me now, would you, sunshine?"

"Absolutely," said the guard.

He never saw the blow that knocked him out. Johnny C smacked him hard with the handle of his revolver, blacking him out in an instant.

"Never fuck with the union," Johnny said.

\* \* \*

Eraser scanned the *Pobyeda* from the roof of a warehouse, counting the Mafia goons parked on the rail of the ship. Holding on to the small shotgun with one hand, he used the other to swing off the roof, shimmying down a drainpipe on the side of the building. As he dropped, he disturbed half a dozen pigeons on a ledge—they took flight suddenly in a cloud of flapping wings. Below him, two guards noticed the birds—then they saw Eraser.

Their weapons came up as Eraser leaped from his perch, landing on the arm of a wrought-iron crane. The guards opened fire, bullets smacking into the hard metal, throwing off sparks. Eraser dropped straight to the ground, his full weight hitting the two guards like a boulder. There was a quick flurry of blows from Eraser and both of the guards were disarmed and incapacitated almost instantly.

Samaritan heard the gunfire and keyed his communication set. "What the hell is going on? Who fired? Report in!" He threw a switch bring up the scene at the main gate. He glimpsed it for a second, then the picture vanished.

"Perimeter check in," Samaritan said frantically. "Perimeter, talk to me goddamned it." He pounded his fist on the console. "EM team, our perimeter has been compromised."

The EM team members fired up the scopes on their weapons. "Copy that," said Calderon.

Calderon, Schiff, and J-Scar scanned the darkness with their weapons, pale green spotlights sweeping the warehouses and shadows looking for targets. Eraser was backed against a warehouse wall, watching as the last container was made ready for lifting off a flatbed truck.

He did not know that J-Scar had locked on him with his X-scope. "Got him," he whispered into his headset. "Thirty yards back." His finger tightened on the trigger. "Bye-bye, asshole."

J-Scar pulled the trigger and unleashed a blazing burst of white-hot flame. Eraser dove for cover as the pulse fire ripped through the walls and windows of the warehouses, blasting through metal and glass. There was a hurricane of deadly shrapnel in the air, blistering fragments that perforated anything left standing.

Calderon and Schiff were firing their EM guns, too. Eraser charged as blazing pulses tore through the air from three different directions. One of the pulses hit a massive turbine wheel and threw it into the air. Two more pulses slammed into two forklifts, which exploded into the air and erupted in flame.

There was panic on the *Pobyeda*. Sergei gave orders for immediate cast off, screaming orders in Russian. He whipped around and glared at Lee.

"It looks as if your friend has arrived," he said. "I wonder if he will make it to the ship alive."

"Oh, he will," said Lee. "I'm going to enjoy introducing him to you. I know he's very anxious to meet you."

Sergei smiled thinly. "I doubt I'll have the pleasure. He has forced me to hasten our departure." He whipped out a long combat knife with a sharp, serrated edge. He grabbed a handful of Lee's hair and pulled her head back, exposing her throat. "And your departure as well."

Lee suddenly jerked on the wire and freed one hand. She grabbed the pot of hot coffee and cracked it across the Russian's face. The glass shattered, slicing into his face and he screamed in agony as the hot liquid boiled his skin. He fell to the deck writhing in agony.

"The pleasure was all mine," said Lee. She untied herself quickly, then bolted for freedom.

**20**

There was a moment of silence as the rail gunners stopped firing. The warehouse was in a shambles, fires burning in piles of debris. Then, slowly, some rubble shifted and Eraser peered out, stunned. He tried to get up, but he couldn't—his leg was trapped in a splintery hole in the old floorboards of the building.

Samaritan stepped out of the command van and looked around, impressed with the destruction the rail guns had wrought.

"Okay," said Samaritan into his headset, "I think it's safe to say we finally got our man."

"I think we even got the cockroaches," J-Scar whispered into his microphone. "All of 'em."

"Now I want some good news," said Samaritan. "Who's still on the ground out there? Royce? Soames? You two alive?"

"I am," said Royce.

"Me, too," said Soames.

"Good. You two are on reconnaissance. EM team back them up." The two guards sprinted for the warehouse. "And get that goddamned container on the move! Now!"

Royce stole into the warehouse like an oily shadow. Eraser heard him coming and tried to extricate his trapped leg, but he was still pinned. He checked his shotgun, the breech and firing pin had been bent and were useless. Eraser thought for a moment and then hurled the shotgun in Royce's direction.

The guard whirled around as the shotgun spun out of the darkness and slid to his feet. Puzzled, he reached down and picked it up, turning it over in his hands, examining it curiously.

In his headset Royce heard J-Scar's voice. "He's not down!" he said excitedly. "I see him. I see his shotgun!"

Royce's eyes opened wide and he jumped. J-Scar was talking about him! "No, wait! Wait!"

A rail-gun blast rocketed through the wall and blasted into Royce's chest. In the scope of J-Scar's rail gun, Royce's skeleton disintegrated, the bones blasting into tiny fragments.

As Royce vaporized, his partner, Soames, rushed forward, his own weapon at the ready. Eraser summoned all his strength and pulled his leg from the hole in the floorboards, shards of wood tearing through his pants, ripping his flesh. Soames heard the noise and advanced—just in time to get nailed. Literally. Eraser drove one of the sharp stakes from the splintered floor deep into the base of the man's neck, severing his spinal column, pinning him to a wooden crossbeam.

Eraser paused long enough to relieve the dead man of a pair of Glock 9mms, then vanished into the crawl space beneath the floor, as Samaritan's voice crackled in Soames's headset.

"Copy recon? Soames? Royce? Do you copy?" Samaritan's good humor vanished. The silence told him all he needed to know. "Alpha team! Secure that entrance! I want my EM gunners in there now!"

Schiff and Calderon broke for the warehouse, but J-Scar was loathe to leave his perch in the control cab of the crane. The container was rising off the flatbed now and J-Scar scanned the area through his scope. Suddenly, he found himself looking at Sal, crouched behind the butt of his rifle.

Before J-Scar could fire, Sal squeezed off a round. The heavy caliber slug went straight through J-Scar's scope, shattering it, then continued on going through J-Scar's eye and out the back of his head. He fell back, his finger tightening on the trigger, blasting away with the rail gun as he died. The control cab was shot to pieces and the container came to an abrupt halt.

Tony and Johnny C looked at Sal with new respect. "That was a pretty good shot," said Johnny C.

"Pretty good?" said Sal indignantly. "It was a fuckin' work of art."

"Well, I wouldn't go that far," said Johnny C.

"Yeah, well, blow me. . . ."

The first thing Calderon and Schiff discovered when they burst into the warehouse was the body of Soames standing upright, impaled by the spike.

"Jesus Christ," Calderon said. "We gotta get this guy."

"Before he gets us," said Schiff.

Suddenly bringing down Eraser wasn't a question of removing an obstacle to a lucrative weapons deal. Now it was a matter of simple survival. The two CIA men looked around the charred warehouse.

"But where the fuck is he?" said Calderon.

Suddenly, the floor beneath their feet was splintered as Eraser fired both Glocks up through the timbers. Schiff and Calderon were riddled with bullets from below as gunshots punched through the timbers. The two men fell, their rail guns clattering on the wooden floor.

As four more men poured into the warehouse, Eraser crashed up from below like some devil rising from hell. He grabbed both rail guns, one in each hand, and blasted away, eradicating the four men, throwing them along the length of the warehouse like flaming human meteors. Explosions from the rail guns ripped out the sides of the warehouse. The air was full of the smell of singed flesh.

"Calderon?" said Samaritan. "Schiff?"

Eraser heard Samaritan's voice coming through Calderon's headset. He stooped and picked it up.

"They missed," he said.

There was a long pause from Samaritan. Then: "Johnny . . . ? Is that you? Where are you, sonny?"

"I'll be right out," Eraser growled.

"Son of a bitch!" Samaritan yelled. "He's still alive. Open fire! Open fire!"

The remaining members of Samaritan's team opened up with everything they had, blasting away, blowing the warehouse to smithereens. But Eraser materialized out of the smoke and flames, both EM guns blazing away. The barrels flashed with each shrieking volley, bright white light strobing in the night.

The command van was blown to pieces, but Samaritan had already abandoned it, scrambling away as his men were blown through the air like weeds. The weapons of the dead men went into good hands—the four mobsters grabbed the Tec-9s and Uzis scattered around and added to the firefight, peppering anything that moved. It had become an all-out war, the Russians firing from the taffrail of the ship, Samaritan's remaining men fighting tenaciously—they were fighting for their lives.

Eraser was in the zone, fighting on automatic pilot, not thinking, just acting. The damage he did with his twin rail guns was awesome. Containers got blasted away as if they weighed no more than shoe boxes; a couple of trucks erupted, thrown into the air like toys. Rail rounds even gouged hunks out of the thick steel plates of the freighter's stout hull.

Then it all stopped. . . .

"John!" Samaritan shouted. Eraser turned and looked through the flames and smoke to see Samaritan and Lee standing on the container, a 9mm pressed against her head. The huge steel box was only eight or ten feet off the ground, swaying slightly like a pendulum.

"Goddamnit, John, now you are pissing me off," Samaritan yelled. "Big time. Now drop the guns. And tell the guineas to do the same."

Eraser hesitated for a moment. Samaritan cocked the Glock. "You're not listening to me, Johnny. I said drop them."

Samaritan made it clear that Eraser had no choice. He tossed the rail guns to the ground and indicated to the mobsters that they should do the same. All over the dock weaponry clattered.

"Thanks," said Samaritan. Then he fired. Two bullets slammed into Eraser, throwing him back, blood erupting from his left thigh and right shoulder. He fell to the ground, pain streaming through him like hot lava. Far off he heard Lee screaming his name.

"Shut up!" Samaritan snapped. "Now would someone get this goddamned crane moving?"

A new operator had climbed into the control cabin and was trying to seat himself without sitting in any of the pools of goo that J-Scar had left behind him. It was not easy—there was a lot of gore in the cab. Finally, he cranked up the engine and engaged the big gears. With a deep rumble the gantry crane started along the tracks toward the ship. As the machine growled forward, the sea container with Samaritan and Lee on top rose slowly.

Through a haze of pain and blood, Eraser saw the crane moving, the cargo container rising. Very slowly he forced himself to his knees. His skin was wet with his own blood and the pain was intense, but he swallowed it, refusing to think about it, forcing the sensation from his mind. With great effort he got to his feet and took a step . . . then another . . . then another. He was gaining momentum. Somehow he reached down into his inner core and found the strength to break into a run. Eraser ran straight for the container.

The metal box was fifteen feet off the ground, but Eraser bounded up a ramp of burning wreckage and launched himself into the air, sailing toward the underside of the container. His superhuman effort was rewarded as he just managed to snag the lower rung of the steel ladder that ran along the side of the cargo carrier.

The entire rig rocked crazily when Eraser hit. Samaritan was unaware that the container had taken on an extra passenger, thinking that the shaky ride was due to incompetence.

"Hey! Take it easy up there," he barked into his headset. He had come this far and had been through so much that he had no intention of checking out now—particularly if it was the result of ineptitude.

Eraser dangled from the ladder for a moment, then hooked the rung with his injured arm and took the next step with his good hand, heaving himself up the side of the container hand over hand, inch by inch.

On the freighter, Sergei saw Eraser clinging to the side of the container. He yelled to his Russian Mafia goons, pointing him out. Soon, automatic weapons' fire started chattering from the ship, spraying bullets all over the place. The moment they started shooting however, Tony Two Toes and Johnny C and the other two mobsters grabbed their discarded weapons and returned fire. Johnny C nailed Sergei with a slug right between the eyes. The gunfire from the ship faltered—then stopped altogether when a well-placed bullet from Little Mike hit some drums of oil on deck and they detonated, huge balls of fire erupting into the night sky.

Samaritan peered over the edge of the container—and a massive, grimy, bloody fist smashed into his face, sending him flying, his gun falling from his hand. The container tilted wildly as Samaritan lunged for his gun, but Lee kicked it away. Eraser hauled himself onto the flat top and rested for a moment. He looked like grim death—a hunched, bloody mess. He was running on sheer will power and guts—and nothing else.

Samaritan shook his head. "Johnny," he said, "you're a wreck. Why don't you just sit quietly there and bleed to death?" Then he launched himself on Eraser, a spinning kick cracking across his face. Eraser responded with a blow to

the gut that rocked Samaritan's world and he fell
back again, the crate spinning.

When he got to his feet, he struck at Eraser's
weakest point. Samaritan ran at Lee and shoved
her hard. She screamed as she flew over the edge
and out into thin air. Eraser made a desperate
lunge for her, catching her, the entire crate rock-
ing wildly. Lee hung in midair as Eraser hauled
her back in with his good arm.

Samaritan used the moment, grabbing a steel
bar from the chain cinch and swinging it down
hard on Eraser's collar bone. The crack of metal
hitting bone was sickening and the pain was
fierce, but Samaritan did not let up. Samaritan
swung the bar again and again, brutally pounding
away at the broken bones.

Mustering one last effort, Eraser smashed Samaritan with a heavy right cross. Samaritan went
cartwheeling back into the hitching cable, catching it at the last second and saving himself.
Samaritan struggled to climb back onto the top
of the container.

Eraser looked to Lee, staring at her through a
haze of blood and sweat. He was breathing hard,
barely able to speak.

"Grab the rung," said Eraser.

"What?"

"Grab the rung."

She followed his eyes upward and saw that as

the container rose, it came close to the ladder mounted on the gantry cab.

"Do it," Eraser urged.

Lee reached up, her fingertips straining, just managing to grab hold of the lowest steel bar.

Samaritan had found his pistol and he leveled it at Eraser. "Say good-bye, John."

Eraser smiled as he reached down and grabbed the steel lever on the side of the container. Samaritan tracked it to the chain hoist assembly and realized it was the release lever.

He paled and his eyes widened. "Oh shit!"

"Good-bye," said Eraser jamming down the lever. Cables unraveled instantly shooting through the gears.

Lee screamed as the surface of the container dropped out from beneath her feet, leaving her dangling. The shipping container fell toward the ground, Samaritan screaming as he and Eraser rode it all the way down, slamming into the dock like the Hammer of God. There was an enormous eruption of shattering wood and steel, rail guns scattering like toothpicks, littering the pier.

When the sound of impact died away, it was replaced with another noise, the chattering of helicopter blades as they slapped the air. A voice boomed from a powerful loudspeaker.

"On the ship! Throw down your arms or we'll open fire!"

Eraser froze as spotlights from above pinned him in place. The air was split by the sound of nautical sirens of two huge Coast Guard cutters slicing across the harbor, bearing down on the *Pobyeda*.

Beller looked down from the helicopter, appalled at what he saw. Samaritan lay semiconscious in the wreckage of the container, surrounded by scattered crates of guns. He looked crushed, defeated . . . the fire had gone out inside him.

Lee rushed up to Eraser and threw her arms around him, tears streaking her face. He leaned into her, both of them battered and weary—and grateful to be alive. They were half blinded by the powerful searchlights and the rotor wash kicked up a roaring storm of turbulent air around them.

Four-wheel drive vehicles came racing on to the pier, heavily armed marshals spilling out, M 16s primed and ready, a firing line with every barrel pointed at Eraser and Lee.

The chopper set down a few yards beyond them and Beller slipped out of the cockpit. He walked toward the shattered container and stopped when he saw the deadly arsenal scattered on the pier.

"What might have happened if this stuff got into the wrong hands?" said Beller. He looked angrily at Eraser. "Get him out of here," he ordered.

Beller and Eraser locked eyes, as the marshals moved in. Eraser was stunned, though, when the law officers walked by him and hauled Samaritan to his feet. They cuffed him, and then they led him away, bruised, bleeding and half dead.

The WITSEC chief looked Eraser straight in the eye. Eraser met the gaze head-on, grim faced.

"I always knew you were my best man," he said.

# 21

The doors of the Federal Courthouse in Washington, D.C., burst open and a sea of spectators, press and lawyers poured out, the crowd buzzing with excitement. Bodyguards and high-priced attorneys flanked Undersecretary Daniel Harper and Samaritan, clearing a path through the crowd of people. Reporters and camera crews swarmed them, microphones jammed into their faces.

"Mr. Undersecretary," a journalist shouted, "how does it feel—a man of your stature indicted for treason?"

"Undersecretary Harper has nothing to say at this time," an attorney barked.

"What about you, Marshal Deguerin?" another reporter shouted.

"I'm proud of what I've done," said Samaritan.

"So you admit to treason?"

"I admit to patriotism," Samaritan announced grandly. "I am not ashamed to have worked for the continued security of the United States of America. If that's a crime, then so be it."

There was another flurry of activity on the courthouse steps. Samaritan and Harper turned to see Morehart and his attorney descending toward a waiting car. Morehart looked over at them and then looked away. Samaritan did not take his eyes off Morehart as he continued to lecture the reporters.

"Let me tell you all about treason," Samaritan said. "Treason is a secret, unholy alliance between certain private interests and some of the nation's worst enemies. That's what we're exposing here. Don't let anyone tell you different. . . ."

Eraser and Lee watched the media circus on the courthouse steps. Eraser wore a sling, his sportcoat draped over his shoulder. The bandage, along with a few superficial cuts and bruises were the only remaining signs of his injuries.

"They could still get away with this, couldn't they?" said Lee.

"If Morehart takes the fall for both of them, they might walk." Eraser paused a moment. "You did well in there."

"I couldn't have done it without you watching over me," said Lee with a soft, affectionate smile.

"I'll always watch over you." Gently, he encircled her neck with a fine gold chain. "We both will."

Lee looked down to see her St. George medallion. Then she looked up at him, surprised and moved.

"Then I guess I'm finally safe," she said.

**H**arper got into the limousine quickly, but Samaritan paused to lob one last volley at the press.

"The public deserves to know the truth," he said. "Today was just a hearing. We look forward to our real day—in court." He ducked into the limousine and slammed the door.

Samaritan sunk into the soft leather seats. "And with any luck, we won't need it. Without Cullen's testimony, there is no trial."

"So," said Harper, "we get rid of her. Tell me your thoughts on that subject, Bob."

"She's gone. It's as good as done."

**E**raser looked down and locked eyes with Samaritan. Then he escorted Lee down the steps to a waiting van from the U.S. Marshals' service. Lee and Eraser stepped inside. The instant the van's engine turned over, the vehicle exploded in an enormous ball of fire, the blast lifting the van straight up in the air, sending it crashing to earth a twisted heap of scorched metal.

Samaritan saw the explosion through the rear window of the limousine as they drove sedately away. He reached into the mini-bar refrigerator, extracted a split of champagne and popped the cork.

"Very good," Samaritan said as he poured some of the golden liquid. "Clean. Swift. Hundreds of witnesses to see we were never near that van. Balls out." He handed a glass to Harper. "I like your style, Danny. It reminds me of . . . well, of me." Samaritan chuckled and drank his champagne.

"My style, Bob?" said Harper, looking a little puzzled. "What do you mean, my style?"

"Damn straight," said Samaritan jovially. "I'd say we're back in business. Wouldn't you."

Harper's hands began to tremble. "You mean you didn't arrange that little exhibition back there?"

"What the hell are you talking about?"

Suddenly, the limousine stopped. Samaritan, distracted, looked through the open partition.

"Hey, Jeeves," he called to the chauffeur. "Let's get a move on here, huh? Why have you stopped?"

The driver just stared at the two men in the rearview mirror. Then, slowly, the smoked glass barrier between the front and back seats whirred shut, cutting them off.

"What the fuck?" Samaritan yelled. Fuming, he hit the intercom button. "You better have a damned good reason. . . ."

The driver's response was to press the button locking all the doors of the long black car. Then he stepped out of the car, took off his sunglasses and smiled at his erstwhile passengers.

" 'Bye," said Johnny C, walking away, leaving the car parked athwart a set of railroad tracks.

Samaritan and Harper fell on the doors, trying to open them. Then they pounded on the windows. Suddenly, the car phone trilled. Harper picked it up, listened for a moment and then handed it to Samaritan.

"It's for you."

Samaritan took the phone and held it to his ear. "You have just been erased," said John Krueger.

Samaritan looked out the window and saw a freight train hurtling toward them, the brakes screaming, the horn blasting. Samaritan had exactly a second to feel pulse-pounding fear. Then the train hit and the limousine blew up, vanishing in a great ball of flame.

Eraser stood in the middle of a private air terminal on the grounds of Dulles International Airport, listening as the static blasted out of the ear piece of his cellular phone, confirmation that

Samaritan and Harper were no longer among the living. He clicked off the phone and put it away, turning in time to see Lee making her way toward him. She was studying a map.

"So," said Lee, "we're really doing this?"

"Looks like it," said Eraser.

"Any second thoughts?"

Eraser nodded. "Yes."

She paused, surprised. Then he leaned down and kissed her softly. They smiled at each other.

"No," he said. "No second thoughts." Eraser glanced at the map. "How about Morocco?"

"Too dry," said Lee.

"Bali?"

"Too wet."

"Katmandu?"

"Do they have cable in Katmandu?" Lee said with a laugh.

Outside the terminal, parked on the tarmac was a Marshals' service Viking, gassed up and ready to go.

"How about Fergus Falls?" said Lee suddenly.

Eraser was intrigued. "Where's that? Let me guess . . . Kenya?"

"Minnesota," said Lee.

"Minnesota."

"Its just outside Fargo," said Lee.

"We can go anywhere in the world," said

Eraser. "And you want to go to Fergus Falls, Minnesota?"

They opened the doors and walked out onto the concrete, making for the small jet.

"We can go to Bali," said Lee. "Someday . . ."

"Yeah." Eraser asked, "When?"

"Next life," said Lee. "Next life."

They paused outside the terminal and looked into the bright blue sky, watching the planes in flight, bound for destinations unknown.